FAIRY TALES

AND FOLK TALES SELECTED
EDITED AND TRANSLATED BY
R. NISBET BAIN

ILLUSTRATED BY
NOEL L. NISBET

ORIGINALLY PUBLISHED BY
GEORGE G. HARRAP & CO.
2 & 3 PORTSMOUTH STREET KINGSWAY W.C.
LONDON
[MCMXVI]

ORIGINALLY PRINTED AT THE COMPLETE PRESS
WEST NORWOOD ENGLAND

RESURRECTED BY
ABELA PUBLISHING, LONDON
[2011]

R. Nisbet Bain

Cossack Fairy Tales

Abela Publishing,
London
United Kingdom
2010

ISBN-13: 978-1-907256-30-1

email Books@AbelaPublishing.com

www.AbelaPublishing.com/cossack.html

ii

ACKNOWLEDGEMENTS

Abela Publishing acknowledges the work that

R. NISBET BAIN

did in translating and publishing

COSSACK FAIRY TALES

in a time well before any electronic media was in use.

* * * * * * *

A percentage of the net profit from the sale of this book

will be donated to charities for educational purposes.

* * * * * * *

YESTERDAYS BOOKS for TODAYS CHARITIES

COSSACK
FAIRY TALES

Uniform with this Volume

RUSSIAN FAIRY TALES

From the Skazki of Polevoi.

By
R. NISBET BAIN.

Illustrated by
NOEL L. NISBET

THEY CAME TO THE PLACE WHERE HE HAD LEFT HER

CONTENTS

ILLUSTRATIONS

INTRODUCTION TO THE FIRST EDITION

THE favourable reception given to my volume of *Russian Fairy Tales* has encouraged me to follow it up with a sister volume of stories selected from another Slavonic dialect extraordinarily rich in folk-tales—I mean Ruthenian, the language of the Cossacks.

Ruthenian is a language intermediate between Russian and Polish, but quite independent of both. Its territory embraces, roughly speaking, that vast plain which lies between the Carpathians, the watershed of the Dnieper, and the Sea of Azov, with Lemberg and Kiev for its chief intellectual centres. Though it has been rigorously repressed by the Russian Government, it is still spoken by more than twenty millions of people. It possesses a noble literature, numerous folk-songs, not inferior even to those of Serbia, and, what chiefly concerns us now, a copious collection of justly admired folk-tales, many of them of great antiquity, which are regarded, both in Russia and Poland, as quite unique of their kind. Mr Ralston, I fancy, was the first to call the attention of the West to these curious stories, though the want at that time of a good Ruthenian dictionary (a want since supplied by the excellent lexicon of Zhelekhovsky and Nidilsky) prevented him from utilizing them. Another Slavonic scholar, Mr Morfill, has also frequently alluded to them in terms of enthusiastic but by no means extravagant praise.

The three chief collections of Ruthenian folk-lore are those of Kulish, Rudchenko, and Dragomanov, which represent, at least approximately, the three dialects into which Ruthenian is generally divided. It is from these three collections that the present selection has been made. Kulish, who has the merit of priority, was little more than a pioneer, his contribution merely consisting of some dozen *kazki* (*Märchen*) and *kazochiki* (*Märchenlein*), incorporated in the second volume of his *Zapiski o yuzhnoi Rusi* ("Descriptions of South Russia," Petrograd, 1856-7). Twelve years later Rudchenko published at Kiev what is still, on the whole, the best collection of Ruthenian folk-tales, under the title of *Narodnuiya Yuzhnorusskiya Skazki* ("Popular South Russian Folk-tales"). Like Linnröt among the Finns, Rudchenko took down the greater part of these tales direct from the lips of the people. In a second volume, published in the following year, he added other stories gleaned from various minor manuscript collections of great rarity. In 1876 the Imperial Russian Geographical Society published at Kiev, under the title of *Malorusskiya Narodnuiya Predonyia i Razkazui* ("Little-Russian Popular Traditions and Tales"), an edition of as many manuscript collections of Ruthenian folk-lore (including poems, proverbs, riddles, and rites) as it could lay its hands upon. This collection, though far less rich in variants than Rudchenko's, contained many original tales which had escaped him, and was ably edited by Michael Dragomanov, by whose name, indeed, it is generally known.

The present attempt to popularize these Cossack stories is, I believe, the first translation ever made from Ruthenian into English. The selection, though naturally restricted, is fairly representative; every variety of folk-tale has a place in it, and it should never be forgotten that the Ruthenian *kazka* (*Märchen*), owing to favourable circumstances, has managed to preserve far more of the fresh spontaneity and naïve simplicity of the primitive folk-tale than her more sophisticated sister, the Russian *skazka*. It is maintained, moreover, by Slavonic scholars that there are peculiar and original elements in these stories not to be found in the folk-lore of other European peoples; such data, for instance, as the magic handkerchiefs (generally beneficial, but sometimes, as in the story of Ivan Golik, terribly baleful), the demon-expelling hemp-and-tar whips, and the magic cattle-teeming egg, so mischievous a possession to the unwary. It may be so, but, after all that Mr Andrew Lang has taught us on the subject, it would be rash for any mere philologist to assert positively that there can be anything really new in folk-lore under the sun. On the other hand, the comparative isolation and primitiveness of the Cossacks, and their remoteness from the great theatres of historical events, would seem to be favourable conditions both for the safe preservation of old myths and the easy development of new ones. It is for professional students of folk-lore to study the original documents for themselves.

R. N. B.

OH: THE TSAR OF THE FOREST

THE olden times were not like the times *we* live in. In the olden times all manner of Evil Powers[1] walked abroad. The world itself was not then as it is now: now there are no such Evil Powers among us. I'll tell you a *kazka*[2] of Oh, the Tsar of the Forest, that you may know what manner of being he was.

Once upon a time, long long ago, beyond the times that we can call to mind, ere yet our great-grandfathers or their grandfathers had been born into the world, there lived a poor man and his wife, and they had one only son, who was not as an only son ought to be to his old father and mother. So idle and lazy was that only son that Heaven help him! He would do nothing, he would not even fetch water from the well, but lay on the stove all day long and rolled among the warm cinders. If they gave him anything to eat, he ate it; and if they didn't give him anything to eat, he did without. His father and mother fretted sorely because of him, and said, "What are we to do with thee, O son? for thou art good for nothing. Other people's children are a stay and a support to their parents, but thou art but a fool and dost consume our bread for naught." But it was of no use at all. He would do nothing but sit on the stove and play with the cinders. So his father and mother grieved over him for many a long day, and at last his mother said to his father, "What is to be done with our son? Thou dost see that he has grown up and yet is of no use to us, and he is so foolish that we can do nothing with him. Look now, if we can send him away, let us send him away; if we can hire him out, let us hire him out; perchance other folk may be able to do more with him than we can." So his father and mother laid their heads together, and sent him to a tailor's to learn tailoring.

1

ALL MANNER OF EVIL POWERS WALKED ABROAD

There he remained three days, but then he ran away home, climbed up on the stove, and again began playing with the cinders. His father then gave him a sound drubbing and sent him to a cobbler's to learn cobbling, but again he ran away home.

His father gave him another drubbing and sent him to a blacksmith to learn smith's work. But there too he did not remain long, but ran away home again, so what was that poor father to do? "I'll tell thee what I'll do with thee, thou son of a dog!" said he. "I'll take thee, thou lazy lout, into another kingdom. There, perchance, they will be able to teach thee better than they can here, and it will be too far for thee to run home." So he took him and set out on his journey.

They went on and on, they went a short way and they went a long way, and at last they came to a forest so dark that they could see neither earth nor sky. They went through this forest, but in a short time they grew very tired, and when they came to a path leading to a clearing full of large tree-stumps, the father said, "I am so tired out that I will rest here a little," and with that he sat down on a tree-stump and cried, "Oh, how tired I am!" He had no sooner said these words than out of the tree-stump, nobody could say how, sprang such a little, little old man, all so wrinkled and puckered, and his beard was quite green and reached right down to his knee.--"What dost thou want of me, O man?" he asked.-- The man was amazed at the strangeness of his coming to light, and said to him, "I did not call thee; begone!"--"How canst thou say that when thou didst call me?" asked the little old man.-- "Who art thou, then?" asked the father.--"I am Oh, the Tsar of the Woods," replied the old man; "why didst thou call me, I say?"-- "Away with thee, I did not call thee," said the man.--"What! thou didst not call me when thou saidst 'Oh'?"--"I was tired, and therefore I said 'Oh'!" replied the man.--"Whither art thou going?" asked Oh.--"The wide world lies before me," sighed the man. "I am taking this sorry blockhead of mine to hire him out to somebody or other. Perchance other people may be able to knock more sense into him than we can at home; but send him whither we will, he always comes running home again!"--"Hire him out to me. I'll warrant I'll teach him," said Oh. "Yet I'll only take him on one condition. Thou shalt come back for him when a year has run, and if thou dost know him again, thou mayst take him; but if thou dost not know him again, he shall serve another year with me."--"Good!" cried the man. So they shook hands upon it, had a good drink to clinch the bargain, and the man went back to his own home, while Oh took the son away with him.

Oh took the son away with him, and they passed into the other world, the world beneath the earth, and came to a green hut woven out of rushes, and in this hut everything was green; the walls were green and the benches were green, and Oh's wife was green and his children were green--in fact, everything there was green. And Oh had water-nixies for serving-maids, and they were all as green as rue. "Sit down now!" said Oh to his new labourer, "and have a bit of something to eat." The nixies then brought him some food, and that also was green, and he ate of it. "And now," said Oh, "take my labourer into the courtyard that he may chop wood and draw water." So they took him into the courtyard, but instead of chopping any wood he lay down and went to sleep. Oh came out to see how he was getting on, and there he lay a-snoring. Then Oh seized him, and bade them bring wood and tie his labourer fast to the wood, and set the wood on fire till the labourer was burnt to ashes. Then Oh took the ashes and scattered them to the four winds, but a single piece of burnt coal fell from out of the ashes, and this coal he sprinkled with living water, whereupon the labourer immediately stood there alive again and somewhat handsomer and stronger than before. Oh again bade him chop wood, but again he went to sleep. Then Oh again tied him to the wood and burnt him and scattered the ashes to the four winds and sprinkled the remnant of the coal with living water, and instead of the loutish clown there stood there such a handsome and stalwart Cossack[3] that the like of him can neither be imagined nor described but only told of in tales.

There, then, the lad remained for a year, and at the end of the year the father came for his son. He came to the self-same charred stumps in the self-same forest, sat him down, and said, "Oh!" Oh immediately came out of the charred stump and said, "Hail! O man!"--"Hail to thee, Oh!"--"And what dost thou want, O man?" asked Oh.--"I have come," said he, "for my son."--"Well, come then! If thou dost know him again, thou shalt take him away; but if thou dost not know him, he shall serve with me yet another year." So the man went with Oh. They came to his hut, and Oh took whole handfuls of millet and scattered it about, and myriads of cocks came running up and pecked it. "Well, dost thou know thy son again?" said Oh. The man stared and stared. There was nothing but cocks, and one cock was just like another. He could not pick out his son. "Well," said Oh, "as thou dost not know him, go home again; this year thy son must remain in my service." So the man went home again.

The second year passed away, and the man again went to Oh. He came to the charred stumps and said, "Oh!" and Oh popped out of the tree-stump again. "Come!" said he, "and see if thou canst recognize him now." Then he took him to a sheep-pen, and there were rows and rows of rams, and one ram was just like another. The man stared and stared, but he could not pick out his son. "Thou mayst as well go home then," said Oh, "but thy son shall live with me yet another year." So the man went away, sad at heart.

The third year also passed away, and the man came again to find Oh. He went on and on till there met him an old man all as white as milk, and the raiment of this old man was glistening white. "Hail to thee, O man!" said he.--"Hail to thee also, my father!"--"Whither doth God lead thee?"--"I am going to free my son from Oh."--"How so?"--Then the man told the old white father how he had hired out his son to Oh and under what conditions.--"Aye, aye!" said the old white father, "'tis a vile pagan thou hast to deal with; he will lead thee about by the nose for a long time."--"Yes," said the man, "I perceive that he is a vile pagan; but I

5

know not what in the world to do with him. Canst thou not tell me then, dear father, how I may recover my son?"--"Yes, I can," said the old man.--"Then prythee tell me, darling father, and I'll pray for thee to God all my life, for though he has not been much of a son to me, he is still my own flesh and blood."--"Hearken, then!" said the old man; "when thou dost go to Oh, he will let loose a multitude of doves before thee, but choose not one of these doves. The dove thou shalt choose must be the one that comes not out, but remains sitting beneath the pear-tree pruning its feathers; that will be thy son." Then the man thanked the old white father and went on.

He came to the charred stumps. "Oh!" cried he, and out came Oh and led him to his sylvan realm. There Oh scattered about handfuls of wheat and called his doves, and there flew down such a multitude of them that there was no counting them, and one dove was just like another. "Dost thou recognize thy son?" asked Oh. "An thou knowest him again, he is thine; an thou knowest him not, he is mine." Now all the doves there were pecking at the wheat, all but one that sat alone beneath the pear-tree, sticking out its breast and pruning its feathers. "That is my son," said the man.--"Since thou hast guessed him, take him," replied Oh. Then the father took the dove, and immediately it changed into a handsome young man, and a handsomer was not to be found in the wide world. The father rejoiced greatly and embraced and kissed him. "Let us go home, my son!" said he. So they went.

As they went along the road together they fell a-talking, and his father asked him how he had fared at Oh's. The son told him. Then the father told the son what he had suffered, and it was the son's turn to listen. Furthermore the father said, "What shall we do now, my son? I am poor and thou art poor: hast thou served these three years and earned nothing?"--"Grieve not, dear dad, all will come right in the end. Look! there are some young nobles hunting after a fox. I will turn myself into a greyhound and catch the fox, then the young noblemen will want to buy me of thee, and thou must sell me to them for three hundred roubles--only, mind thou sell me without a chain; then we shall have lots of money at home, and will live happily together!"

They went on and on, and there, on the borders of a forest, some hounds were chasing a fox. They chased it and chased it, but the fox kept on escaping, and the hounds could not run it down. Then the son changed himself into a greyhound, and ran down the fox and killed it. The noblemen thereupon came galloping out of the forest. "Is that thy greyhound?"--"It is."--"'Tis a good dog; wilt sell it to us?"--"Bid for it!"--"What dost thou require?"--"Three hundred roubles without a chain."--"What do we want with *thy* chain, we would give him a chain of gold. Say a hundred roubles!"--"Nay!"--"Then take thy money and give us the dog." They counted down the money and took the dog and set off hunting. They sent the dog after another fox. Away he went after it and chased it right into the forest, but then he turned into a youth again and rejoined his father.

They went on and on, and his father said to him, "What use is this money to us after all? It is barely enough to begin housekeeping with and repair our hut."--"Grieve not, dear dad, we shall get more still. Over yonder are some young noblemen hunting quails with falcons. I will change myself into a falcon, and thou must sell me to them; only sell me for three hundred roubles, and without a hood."

They went into the plain, and there were some young noblemen casting their falcon at a quail. The falcon pursued but always fell short of the quail, and the quail always eluded the falcon. The son then changed himself into a falcon and immediately struck down its prey. The young noblemen saw it and were astonished. "Is that thy falcon?"--"'Tis mine."--"Sell it to us, then!"--"Bid for it!"-- "What dost thou want for it?"--"If ye give three hundred roubles, ye may take it, but it must be without the hood."--"As if we want *thy* hood! We'll make for it a hood worthy of a Tsar." So they higgled and haggled, but at last they gave him the three hundred roubles. Then the young nobles sent the falcon after another quail, and it flew and flew till it beat down its prey; but then he became a youth again, and went on with his father.

"How shall we manage to live with so little?" said the father.--"Wait a while, dad, and we shall have still more," said the son. "When we pass through the fair I'll change myself into a horse, and thou must sell me. They will give thee a thousand roubles for me, only sell me without a halter." So when they got to the next little town, where they were holding a fair, the son changed himself into a horse, a horse as supple as a serpent, and so fiery that it was dangerous to approach him. The father led the horse along by the halter; it pranced about and struck sparks from the ground with its hoofs. Then the horse-dealers came together and began to bargain for it. "A thousand roubles down," said he, "and you may have it, but without the halter."--"What do we want with *thy* halter? We will make for it a silver-gilt halter. Come, we'll give thee five hundred!"--"No!" said he. Then up there came a gipsy, blind of one eye. "O man! what dost thou want for that horse?" said he.--"A thousand roubles without the halter."--"Nay! but that is dear, little father! Wilt thou not take five hundred with the halter?"--"No, not a bit of it!"--"Take six hundred, then!" Then the gipsy began higgling and haggling, but the man would not give way. "Come, sell it," said he, "with the halter."--"No, thou gipsy, I have a liking for that halter."--"But, my good man, when didst thou ever see them sell a horse without a halter? How then can one lead him off?"--"Nevertheless, the halter must remain mine."--"Look now, my father, I'll give thee five roubles extra, only I must have the halter."--The old man fell a-thinking. "A halter of this kind is worth but three *grivni*[4] and the gipsy offers me five roubles for it; let him have it." So they clinched the bargain with a good drink, and the old man went home with the money, and the gipsy walked off with the horse. But it was not really a gipsy, but Oh, who had taken the shape of a gipsy.

Then Oh rode off on the horse, and the horse carried him higher than the trees of the forest, but lower than the clouds of the sky.

At last they sank down among the woods and came to Oh's hut, and Oh went into his hut and left his horse outside on the steppe. "This son of a dog shall not escape from my hands so quickly a second time," said he to his wife. At dawn Oh took the horse by the bridle and led it away to the river to water it.

But no sooner did the horse get to the river and bend down its head to drink than it turned into a perch and began swimming away. Oh, without more ado, turned himself into a pike and pursued the perch. But just as the pike was almost up with it, the perch gave a sudden twist and stuck out its spiky fins and turned its tail toward the pike, so that the pike could not lay hold of it. So when the pike came up to it, it said, "Perch! perch! turn thy head toward me, I want to have a chat with thee!"--"I can hear thee very well as I am, dear cousin, if thou art inclined to chat," said the perch. So off they set again, and again the pike overtook the perch. "Perch! perch! turn thy head round toward me, I want to have a chat with thee!" Then the perch stuck out its bristly fins again and said, "If thou dost wish to have a chat, dear cousin, I can hear thee just as well as I am." So the pike kept on pursuing the perch, but it was of no use. At last the perch swam ashore, and there was a Tsarivna[5] whittling an ash twig. The perch changed itself into a gold ring set with garnets, and the Tsarivna saw it and fished up the ring out of the water. Full of joy she took it home, and said to her father, "Look, dear papa! what a nice ring I have found!" The Tsar kissed her, but the Tsarivna did not know which finger it would suit best, it was so lovely.

About the same time they told the Tsar that a certain merchant had come to the palace. It was Oh, who had changed himself into a merchant. The Tsar went out to him and said, "What dost thou want, old man?"--"I was sailing on the sea in my ship," said Oh, "and carrying to the Tsar of my own land a precious garnet ring, and this ring I dropped into the water. Has any of thy servants perchance found this precious ring?"--"No, but my daughter has," said the Tsar.

"HOW MUCH DO YOU WANT FOR THAT HORSE?"

So they called the damsel, and Oh began to beg her to give it back to him, "for I may not live in this world if I bring not the ring," said he. But it was of no avail, she would not give it up.

Then the Tsar himself spoke to her. "Nay, but, darling daughter, give it up, lest misfortune befall this man because of us; give it up, I say!" Then Oh begged and prayed her yet more, and said, "Take what thou wilt of me, only give me back the ring."--"Nay, then," said the Tsarivna, "it shall be neither mine nor thine," and with that she tossed the ring upon the ground, and it turned into a heap of millet-seed and scattered all about the floor. Then Oh, without more ado, changed into a cock, and began pecking up all the seed. He pecked and pecked till he had pecked it all up. Yet there was one single little grain of millet which rolled right beneath the feet of the Tsarivna, and that he did not see. When he had done pecking he got upon the window-sill, opened his wings, and flew right away.

But the one remaining grain of millet-seed turned into a most beauteous youth, a youth so beauteous that when the Tsarivna beheld him she fell in love with him on the spot, and begged the Tsar and Tsaritsa right piteously to let her have him as her husband. "With no other shall I ever be happy," said she; "my happiness is in him alone!" For a long time the Tsar wrinkled his brows at the thought of giving his daughter to a simple youth; but at last he gave them his blessing, and they crowned them with bridal wreaths, and all the world was bidden to the wedding-feast. And I too was there, and drank beer and mead, and what my mouth could not hold ran down over my beard, and my heart rejoiced within me.

R. Nisbet Bain

THE STORY OF THE WIND

ONCE upon a time there dwelt two brethren in one village, and one brother was very, very rich, and the other brother was very, very poor. The rich man had wealth of all sorts, but all that the poor man had was a heap of children.

One day, at harvest-time, the poor man left his wife and went to reap and thresh out his little plot of wheat, but the Wind came and swept all his corn away down to the very last grain. The poor man was exceeding wrath thereat, and said, "Come what will, I'll go seek the Wind, and I'll tell him with what pains and trouble I had got my corn to grow and ripen, and then he, forsooth! must needs come and blow it all away."

So the man went home and made ready to go, and as he was making ready his wife said to him, "Whither away, husband?"-- "I am going to seek the Wind," said he; "what dost thou say to that?"--"I should say, do no such thing," replied his wife. "Thou knowest the saying, 'If thou dost want to find the Wind, seek him on the open steppe. He can go ten different ways to thy one.' Think of that, dear husband, and go not at all."--"I mean to go," replied the man, "though I never return home again." Then he took leave of his wife and children, and went straight out into the wide world to seek the Wind on the open steppe.

He went on farther and farther till he saw before him a forest, and on the borders of that forest stood a hut on hens' legs. The man went into this hut and was filled with astonishment, for there lay on the floor a huge, huge old man, as grey as milk. He lay there stretched at full length, his head on the seat of honour,[6] with an arm and leg in each of the four corners, and all his hair standing on end. It was no other than the Wind himself.

THE WIND CAME AND SWEPT ALL HIS CORN AWAY

The man stared at this awful Ancient with terror, for never in his life had he seen anything like it. "God help thee, old father!" cried he.--"Good health to thee, good man!" said the ancient giant, as he lay on the floor of the hut. Then he asked him in the most friendly manner, "Whence hath God brought thee hither, good man?"--"I am wandering through the wide world in search of the Wind," said the man. "If I find him, I will turn back; if I don't find him, I shall go on and on till I do."--"What dost thou want with the Wind?" asked the old giant lying on the floor. "Or what wrong hath he done thee, that thou shouldst seek him out so doggedly?"--"What wrong hath he done me?" replied the wayfarer. "Hearken now, O Ancient, and I will tell thee! I went straight from my wife into the field and reaped my little plot of corn; but when I began to thresh it out, the Wind came and caught and scattered every bit of it in a twinkling, so that there was not a single little grain of it left. So now thou dost see, old man, what I have to thank him for. Tell me, in God's name, why such things be? My little plot of corn was my all-in-all, and in the sweat of my brow did I reap and thresh it; but the Wind came and blew it all away, so that not a trace of it is to be found in the wide world. Then I thought to myself, 'Why should he do this?' And I said to my wife, 'I'll go seek the Wind, and say to him, "Another time, visit not the poor man who hath but a little corn, and blow it not away, for bitterly doth he rue it!"'"--"Good, my son!" said the giant who lay on the floor. "I shall know better in future; in future I will not blow away the poor man's corn. But, good man, there is no need for thee to seek the Wind in the open steppe, for I myself am the Wind."--"Then if thou art the Wind," said the man, "give me back my corn."--"Nay," said the giant; "thou canst not make the dead come back from the grave. Yet, inasmuch as I have done thee a mischief, I will now give thee this sack, good man, and do thou take it home with thee. And whenever thou wantest a meal say, 'Sack, sack, give me to eat and drink!' and immediately thou shalt have thy fill both of meat and drink, so now thou wilt have wherewithal to comfort thy wife and children."

Then the man was full of gratitude. "I thank thee, O Wind!" said he, "for thy courtesy in giving me such a sack as will give me my fill of meat and drink without the trouble of working for it."-- "For a lazy loon, 'twere a double boon," said the Wind. "Go home, then, but look now, enter no tavern by the way; I shall know it if thou dost."--"No," said the man, "I will not." And then he took leave of the Wind and went his way.

He had not gone very far when he passed by a tavern, and he felt a burning desire to find out whether the Wind had spoken the truth in the matter of the sack. "How can a man pass a tavern without going into it?" thought he; "I'll go in, come what may. The Wind won't know, because he can't see." So he went into the tavern and hung up his sack upon a peg. The Jew who kept the tavern immediately said to him, "What dost thou want, good man?"--"What is that to thee, thou dog?" said the man.--"You are all alike," sneered the Jew, "take what you can, and pay for nothing."--"Dost think I want to buy anything from thee?" shrieked the man; then, turning angrily to the sack, he cried, "Sack, sack, give me to eat and drink!" Immediately the table was covered with all sorts of meats and liquors. Then all the Jews in the tavern crowded round full of amazement, and asked all manner of questions. "Why, what is this, good man?" said they; "never have we seen anything like this before!"--"Ask no questions, ye accursed Jews!" cried the man, "but sit down to eat, for there is enough for all." So the Jews and the Jewesses set to and ate until they were full up to the ears; and they drank the man's health in pitchers of wine of every sort, and said, "Drink, good man, and spare not, and when thou hast drunk thy fill thou shalt lodge with us this night. We'll make ready a bed for thee. None shall vex thee. Come now, eat and drink whatever thy soul desires." So the Jews flattered him with devilish cunning, and almost forced the wine-jars to his lips.

The simple fellow did not perceive their malice and cunning, and he got so drunk that he could not move from the place, but went to sleep where he was. Then the Jews changed his sack for another, which they hung up on a peg, and then they woke him. "Dost hear, fellow!" cried they; "get up, it is time to go home. Dost thou not see the morning light?" The man sat up and scratched the back of his head, for he was loath to go. But what was he to do? So he shouldered the sack that was hanging on the peg, and went off home.

When he got to his house, he cried, "Open the door, wife!" Then his wife opened the door, and he went in and hung his sack on the peg and said, "Sit down at the table, dear wife, and you children sit down there too. Now, thank God! we shall have enough to eat and drink, and to spare." The wife looked at her husband and smiled. She thought he was mad, but down she sat, and her children sat down all round her, and she waited to see what her husband would do next. Then the man said, "Sack, sack, give to us meat and drink!" But the sack was silent. Then he said again, "Sack, sack, give my children something to eat!" And still the sack was silent. Then the man fell into a violent rage. "Thou didst give me something at the tavern," cried he; "and now I may call in vain. Thou givest nothing, and thou hearest nothing"--and, leaping from his seat, he took up a club and began beating the sack till he had knocked a hole in the wall, and beaten the sack to bits. Then he set off to seek the Wind again. But his wife stayed at home and put everything to rights again, railing and scolding at her husband as a madman.

But the man went to the Wind and said, "Hail to thee, O Wind!"-- "Good health to thee, O man!" replied the Wind. Then the Wind asked, "Wherefore hast thou come hither, O man? Did I not give thee a sack? What more dost thou want?"--"A pretty sack indeed!" replied the man; "that sack of thine has been the cause of much mischief to me and mine."--"What mischief has it done thee?"--"Why, look now, old father, I'll tell thee what it has done. It wouldn't give me anything to eat and drink, so I began beating it, and beat the wall in. Now what shall I do to repair my crazy hut? Give me something, old father."--But the Wind replied, "Nay, O man, thou must do without. Fools are neither sown nor reaped, but grow of their own accord--hast thou not been into a tavern?"--"I have not," said the man.--"Thou hast not? Why wilt thou lie?"--"Well, and suppose I did lie?" said the man; "if thou suffer harm through thine own fault, hold thy tongue about it, that's what I say. Yet it is all the fault of thy sack that this evil has come upon me. If it had only given me to eat and to drink, I should not have come to thee again." At this the Wind scratched his head a bit, but then he said, "Well then, thou man! there's a little ram for thee, and whenever thou dost want money say to it, 'Little ram, little ram, scatter money!' and it will scatter money as much as thou wilt. Only bear this in mind: go not into a tavern, for if thou dost, I shall know all about it; and if thou comest to me a third time, thou shalt have cause to remember it forever."--"Good," said the man, "I won't go."--Then he took the little ram, thanked the Wind, and went on his way.

So the man went along leading the little ram by a string, and they came to a tavern, that very same tavern where he had been before, and again a strong desire came upon the man to go in. So he stood by the door and began thinking whether he should go in or not, and whether he had any need to find out the truth about the little ram. "Well, well," said he at last, "I'll go in, only this time I won't get drunk. I'll drink just a glass or so, and then I'll go home." So into the tavern he went, dragging the little ram after him, for he was afraid to let it go.

Now, when the Jews who were inside there saw the little ram, they began shrieking and said, "What art thou thinking of, O man! that thou bringest that little ram into the room? Are there no barns outside where thou mayst put it up?"--"Hold your tongues, ye accursed wretches!" replied the man; "what has it got to do with you? It is not the sort of ram that fellows like you deal in. And if you don't believe me, spread a cloth on the floor and you shall see something, I warrant you."--Then he said, "Little ram, little ram, scatter money!" and the little ram scattered so much money that it seemed to grow, and the Jews screeched like demons.--"O man, man!" cried they, "such a ram as that we have never seen in all our days. Sell it to us! We will give thee such a lot of money for it."--"You may pick up all that money, ye accursed ones," cried the man, "but I don't mean to sell my ram."

Then the Jews picked up the money, but they laid before him a table covered with all the dishes that a man's heart may desire, and they begged him to sit down and make merry, and said with true Jewish cunning, "Though thou mayst get a little lively, don't get drunk, for thou knowest how drink plays the fool with a man's wits."--The man marvelled at the straightforwardness of the Jews in warning him against the drink, and, forgetting everything else, sat down at table and began drinking pot after pot of mead, and talking with the Jews, and his little ram went clean out of his head. But the Jews made him drunk, and laid him in the bed, and changed rams with him; his they took away, and put in its place one of their own exactly like it.

When the man had slept off his carouse, he arose and went away, taking the ram with him, after bidding the Jews farewell. When he got to his hut he found his wife in the doorway, and the moment she saw him coming, she went into the hut and cried to her children, "Come, children! make haste, make haste! for daddy is coming, and brings a little ram along with him; get up, and look sharp about it! An evil year of waiting has been the lot of wretched me, but he has come home at last."

The husband arrived at the door and said, "Open the door, little wife; open, I say!"--The wife replied, "Thou art not a great nobleman, so open the door thyself. Why dost thou get so drunk that thou dost not know how to open a door? It's an evil time that I spend with thee. Here we are with all these little children, and yet thou dost go away and drink."--Then the wife opened the door, and the husband walked into the hut and said, "Good health to thee, dear wife!"--But the wife cried, "Why dost thou bring that ram inside the hut, can't it stay outside the walls?"-- "Wife, wife!" said the man, "speak, but don't screech. Now we shall have all manner of good things, and the children will have a fine time of it."--"What!" said the wife, "what good can we get from that wretched ram? Where shall we get the money to find food for it? Why, we've nothing to eat ourselves, and thou dost saddle us with a ram besides. Stuff and nonsense! I say."--"Silence, wife," replied the husband; "that ram is not like other rams, I tell thee."--"What sort is it, then?" asked his wife.--"Don't ask questions, but spread a cloth on the floor and keep thine eyes open."--"Why spread a cloth?" asked the wife.--"Why?" shrieked the man in a rage; "do what I tell thee, and hold thy tongue."--But the wife said, "Alas, alas! I have an evil time of it. Thou dost nothing at all but go away and drink, and then thou comest home and dost talk nonsense, and bringest sacks and rams with thee, and knockest down our little hut."--At this the husband could control his rage no longer, but shrieked at the ram, "Little ram, little ram, scatter money!"--But the ram only stood there and stared at him. Then he cried again, "Little ram, little ram, scatter money!"--But the ram stood there stock-still and did nothing. Then the man in his anger caught up a piece of wood and struck the ram on the head, but the poor ram only uttered a feeble baa! and fell to the earth dead.

The man was now very much offended and said, "I'll go to the Wind again, and I'll tell him what a fool he has made of me." Then he took up his hat and went, leaving everything behind him. And the poor wife put everything to rights, and reproached and railed at her husband.

So the man came to the Wind for the third time and said, "Wilt thou tell me, please, if thou art really the Wind or no?"--"What's the matter with thee?" asked the Wind.--"I'll tell thee what's the matter," said the man; "why hast thou laughed at and mocked me and made such a fool of me?"--"I laugh at *thee*!" thundered the old father as he lay there on the floor and turned round on the other ear; "why didst thou not hold fast what I gave thee? Why didst thou not listen to me when I told thee not to go into the tavern, eh?"--"What tavern dost thou mean?" asked the man proudly; "as for the sack and the ram thou didst give me, they only did me a mischief; give me something else."--"What's the use of giving thee anything?" said the Wind; "thou wilt only take it to the tavern. Out of the drum, my twelve henchmen!" cried the Wind, "and just give this accursed drunkard a good lesson that he may keep his throat dry and listen a little more to old people!"-- Immediately twelve henchmen leaped out of his drum and began giving the man a sound thrashing. Then the man saw that it was no joke and begged for mercy. "Dear old father Wind," cried he, "be merciful, and let me get off alive. I'll not come to thee again though I should have to wait till the Judgment Day, and I'll do all thy behests."--"Into the drum, my henchmen!" cried the Wind.-- "And now, O man!" said the Wind, "thou mayst have this drum with the twelve henchmen, and go to those accursed Jews, and if they will not give thee back thy sack and thy ram, thou wilt know what to say."

So the man thanked the Wind for his good advice, and went on his way. He came to the inn, and when the Jews saw that he brought nothing with him they said, "Hearken, O man! don't come here, for we have no brandy."--"What do I want with your brandy?" cried the man in a rage.--"Then for what hast thou come hither?"--"I have come for my own."--"Thy own," said the Jews; "what dost thou mean?"--"What do I mean?" roared the man; "why, my sack and my ram, which you must give up to me."--"What ram? What sack?" said the Jews; "why, thou didst take them away from here thyself."--"Yes, but you changed them," said the man.--"What dost thou mean by changed?" whined the Jews; "we will go before the magistrate, and thou shalt hear from us about this."--"You will have an evil time of it if you go before the magistrate," said the man; "but at any rate, give me back my own."

"OUT OF THE DRUM, MY HENCHMEN!"

And he sat down upon a bench. Then the Jews caught him by the shoulders to cast him out and cried, "Be off, thou rascal! Does any one know where this man comes from? No doubt he is an evil-doer." The man could not stand this, so he cried, "Out of the drum, my henchmen! and give the accursed Jews a sound drubbing, that they may know better than to take in honest folk!" and immediately the twelve henchmen leaped out of the drum and began thwacking the Jews finely.--"Oh, oh!" roared the Jews; "oh, dear, darling, good man, we'll give thee whatever thou dost want, only leave off beating us! Let us live a bit longer in the world, and we will give thee back everything."--"Good!" said the man, "and another time you'll know better than to deceive people." Then he cried, "Into the drum, my henchmen!" and the henchmen disappeared, leaving the Jews more dead than alive. Then they gave the man his sack and his ram, and he went home, but it was a long, long time before the Jews forgot those henchmen.

So the man went home, and his wife and children saw him coming from afar. "Daddy is coming home now with a sack and a ram!" said she; "what shall we do? We shall have a bad time of it, we shall have nothing left at all. God defend us poor wretches! Go and hide everything, children." So the children hastened away, but the husband came to the door and said, "Open the door!"--"Open the door thyself," replied the wife.--Again the husband bade her open the door, but she paid no heed to him. The man was astonished. This was carrying a joke too far, so he cried to his henchmen, "Henchmen, henchmen! out of the drum, and teach my wife to respect her husband!" Then the henchmen leaped out of the drum, laid the good wife by the heels, and began to give her a sound drubbing. "Oh, my dear, darling husband!" shrieked the wife, "never to the end of my days will I be sulky with thee again. I'll do whatever thou tellest me, only leave off beating me."--"Then I have taught thee sense, eh?" said the man.--"Oh, yes, yes, good husband!" cried she. Then the man said: "Henchmen,

23

henchmen! into the drum!" and the henchmen leaped into it again, leaving the poor wife more dead than alive.

Then the husband said to her, "Wife, spread a cloth upon the floor." The wife scudded about as nimbly as a fly, and spread a cloth out on the floor without a word. Then the husband said, "Little ram, little ram, scatter money!" And the little ram scattered money till there were piles and piles of it. "Pick it up, my children," said the man, "and thou too, wife, take what thou wilt!"--And they didn't wait to be asked twice. Then the man hung up his sack on a peg and said, "Sack, sack, meat and drink!" Then he caught hold of it and shook it, and immediately the table was as full as it could hold with all manner of victuals and drink. "Sit down, my children, and thou too, dear wife, and eat thy fill. Thank God, we shall now have no lack of food, and shall not have to work for it either."

So the man and his wife were very happy together, and were never tired of thanking the Wind. They had not had the sack and the ram very long when they grew very rich, and then the husband said to the wife, "I tell thee what, wife!"--"What?" said she.--"Let us invite my brother to come and see us."--"Very good," she replied; "invite him, but dost thou think he'll come?"--"Why shouldn't he?" asked her husband. "Now, thank God, we have everything we want. He wouldn't come to us when we were poor and he was rich, because then he was ashamed to say that I was his brother, but now even he hasn't got so much as we have."

So they made ready, and the man went to invite his brother. The poor man came to his rich brother and said, "Hail to thee, brother; God help thee!"--Now the rich brother was threshing wheat on his threshing-floor, and, raising his head, was surprised to see his brother there, and said to him haughtily, "I thank thee. Hail to thee also! Sit down, my brother, and tell us why thou hast come hither."--"Thanks, my brother, I do not want to sit down. I have come hither to invite thee to us, thee and thy wife."--"Wherefore?" asked the rich brother.--The poor man said, "My wife prays thee, and I pray thee also, to come and dine with us of thy courtesy."--"Good!" replied the rich brother, smiling secretly. "I will come whatever thy dinner may be."

So the rich man went with his wife to the poor man, and already from afar they perceived that the poor man had grown rich. And the poor man rejoiced greatly when he saw his rich brother in his house. And his tongue was loosened, and he began to show him everything, whatsoever he possessed. The rich man was amazed that things were going so well with his brother, and asked him how he had managed to get on so. But the poor man answered, "Don't ask me, brother. I have more to show thee yet." Then he took him to his copper money, and said, "There are my oats, brother!" Then he took and showed him his silver money, and said, "That's the sort of barley I thresh on my threshing-floor!" And, last of all, he took him to his gold money, and said, "There, my dear brother, is the best wheat I've got."--Then the rich brother shook his head, not once nor twice, and marvelled at the sight of so many good things, and he said, "Wherever didst thou pick up all this, my brother?"--"Oh! I've more than that to show thee yet. Just be so good as to sit down on that chair, and I'll show and tell thee everything."

Then they sat them down, and the poor man hung up his sack upon a peg. "Sack, sack, meat and drink!" he cried, and immediately the table was covered with all manner of dishes. So they ate and ate, till they were full up to the ears. When they had eaten and drunken their fill, the poor man called to his son to bring the little ram into the hut. So the lad brought in the ram, and the rich brother wondered what they were going to do with it. Then the poor man said, "Little ram, scatter money!" And the little ram scattered money, till there were piles and piles of it on the floor. "Pick it up!" said the poor man to the rich man and his wife. So they picked it up, and the rich brother and his wife marvelled, and the brother said, "Thou hast a very nice piece of goods there, brother. If I had only something like that I should lack nothing;" then, after thinking a long time, he said, "Sell it to me, my brother."--"No," said the poor man, "I will not sell it."--After a little time, however, the rich brother said again, "Come now! I'll give thee for it six yoke of oxen, and a plough, and a harrow, and a hay-fork, and I'll give thee besides, lots of corn to sow, thus thou wilt have plenty, but give me the ram and the sack." So at last they exchanged. The rich man took the sack and the ram, and the poor man took the oxen and went out to the plough.

Then the poor brother went out ploughing all day, but he neither watered his oxen nor gave them anything to eat. And next day the poor brother again went out to his oxen, but found them rolling on their sides on the ground. He began to pull and tug at them, but they didn't get up. Then he began to beat them with a stick, but they uttered not a sound. The man was surprised to find them fit for nothing, and off he ran to his brother, not forgetting to take with him his drum with the henchmen.

When the poor brother came to the rich brother's, he lost no time in crossing his threshold, and said, "Hail, my brother!"--"Good health to thee also!" replied the rich man, "why hast thou come hither? Has thy plough broken, or thy oxen failed thee? Perchance thou hast watered them with foul water, so that their blood is stagnant, and their flesh inflamed?"--"The murrain take 'em if I know thy meaning!" cried the poor brother. "All that I know is that I thwacked 'em till my arms ached, and they wouldn't stir, and not a single grunt did they give; till I was so angry that I spat at them, and came to tell thee. Give me back my sack and my ram, I say, and take back thy oxen, for they won't listen to me!"--"What! take them back!" roared the rich brother. "Dost think I only made the exchange for a single day? No, I gave them to thee once and for all, and now thou wouldst rip the whole thing up like a goat at the fair. I have no doubt thou hast neither watered them nor fed them, and that is why they won't stand up."--"I didn't know," said the poor man, "that oxen needed water and food."--"Didn't know!" screeched the rich man, in a mighty rage, and taking the poor brother by the hand, he led him away from the hut. "Go away," said he, "and never come back here again, or I'll have thee hanged on a gallows!"--"Ah! what a big gentleman we are!" said the poor brother; "just thou give me back my own, and then I will go away."--"Thou hadst better not stop here," said the rich brother; "come, stir thy stumps, thou pagan! Go home ere I beat thee!"--"Don't say that," replied the poor man, "but give me back my ram and my sack, and then I *will* go."--At this the rich brother quite lost his temper, and cried to his wife and children, "Why do you stand staring like that? Can't you come and help me to pitch this insolent rogue out of the house?" This, however, was something beyond a joke, so the poor brother called to his henchmen, "Henchmen, henchmen! out of the drum, and give this brother of mine and his wife a sound drubbing, that they may think twice about it another time before they pitch a poor brother out of their hut!" Then the henchmen leaped out of the drum, and laid hold of the rich brother and his wife, and trounced them soundly, until the rich brother yelled with all his might, "Oh, oh! my own true brother, take what thou wilt, only let me off alive!" whereupon the poor brother cried to his henchmen, "Henchmen, henchmen! into the drum!" and the henchmen disappeared immediately.

Then the poor brother took his ram and his sack, and set off home with them. And they lived happily ever after, and grew richer and richer. They sowed neither wheat nor barley, and yet they had lots and lots to eat. And I was there, and drank mead and beer. What my mouth couldn't hold ran down my beard. For you, there's a *kazka*, but there be fat hearth-cakes for me the asker. And if I have aught to eat, thou shalt share the treat.

R. Nisbet Bain

THE VOICES AT THE WINDOW

A NOBLEMAN went hunting one autumn, and with him went a goodly train of huntsmen. All day long they hunted and hunted, and at the end of the day they had caught nothing. At last dark night overtook them. It had now grown bitterly cold, and the rain began to fall heavily. The nobleman was wet to the skin, and his teeth chattered. He rubbed his hands together and cried, "Oh, had we but a warm hut, and a white bed, and soft bread, and sour kvas,[7] we should have naught to complain of, but would tell tales and feign fables till dawn of day!" Immediately there shone a light in the depths of the forest. They hastened up to it, and lo! there was a hut. They entered, and on the table lay bread and a jug of kvas; and the hut was warm, and the bed therein was white--everything just as the nobleman had desired it. So they all entered after him, and said grace, and had supper, and laid them down to sleep.

They all slept, all but one, but to him slumber would not come. About midnight he heard a strange noise, and something came to the window and said, "Oh, thou son of a dog! thou didst say, 'If we had but a warm hut, and a white bed, and soft bread, and sour kvas, we should have naught to complain of, but would tell tales and feign fables till dawn'; but now thou hast forgotten thy fine promise! Wherefore this shall befall thee on thy way home. Thou shalt fall in with an apple-tree full of apples, and thou shalt desire to taste of them, and when thou hast tasted thereof thou shalt burst. And if any of these thy huntsmen hear this thing and tell thee of it, that man shall become stone to the knee!" All this that huntsman heard, and he thought, "Woe is me!"

29

And about the second cockcrow something else came to the window and said, "Oh, thou son of a dog! thou didst say, 'If we had but a warm hut, and a white bed, and soft bread, and sour kvas, we should have naught to complain of, but would tell tales and feign fables till dawn'; but now thou hast forgotten thy fine promises! Wherefore this shall befall thee on thy way home. Thou shalt come upon a spring by the roadside, a spring of pure water, and thou shalt desire to drink of it, and when thou hast drunk thereof thou shalt burst. But if any of these thy huntsmen hear and tell thee of this thing, he shall become stone to the girdle." All this that huntsman heard, and he thought to himself, "Woe is me!"

Again, toward the third cockcrow, he heard something else coming to the window, and it said, "Oh, thou son of a dog! thou didst say, 'If only we had a warm hut, and a white bed, and soft bread, and sour kvas, we should have naught to complain of, but would tell tales and feign fables till dawn'; but now thou hast forgotten all thy fine promises! Wherefore this shall befall thee on thy way home. Thou shalt come upon a feather-bed in the highway; a longing for rest shall come over thee, and thou wilt lie down on it, and the moment thou liest down thereon thou shalt burst. But if any of thy huntsmen hear this thing and tell it thee, he shall become stone up to the neck!" All this that huntsman heard, and then he awoke his comrades and said, "It is time to depart!"--"Let us go then," said the nobleman.

So on they went, and they had not gone very far when they saw an apple-tree growing by the wayside, and on it were apples so beautiful that words cannot describe them. The nobleman felt that he must taste of these apples or die; but the wakeful huntsman rushed up and cut down the apple-tree, whereupon apples and apple-tree turned to ashes. But the huntsman galloped on before and hid himself.

They went on a little farther till they came to a spring, and the water of that spring was so pure and clear that words cannot describe it. Then the nobleman felt that he must drink of that water or die; but the huntsman rushed up and splashed in the spring with his sword, and immediately the water turned to blood. The nobleman was wrath, and cried, "Cut me down that son of a dog!" But the huntsman rode on in front and hid himself.

They went on still farther till they came upon a golden bed in the highway, full of white feathers so soft and cosy that words cannot describe it. The nobleman felt that he must rest in that bed or die. Then the huntsman rushed up and struck the bed with his sword, and it turned to coal. But the nobleman was very wrath, and cried, "Shoot me down that son of a dog!" But the huntsman rode on before and hid himself.

When they got home the nobleman commanded them to bring the huntsman before him. "What hast thou done, thou son of Satan?" he cried. "I must needs slay thee!" But the huntsman said, "My master, bid them bring hither into the courtyard an old mare fit for naught but the knacker." They brought the mare, and he mounted it and said, "My master, last midnight something came beneath the window and said, 'Oh, son of a dog! thou saidst, "If only we had a warm hut, and a white bed, and soft bread, and sour kvas, we should grieve no more, but tell tales and feign fables till dawn," and now thou hast forgotten thy promise. Wherefore this shall befall thee on thy way home: thou shalt come upon an apple-tree covered with apples by the wayside, and straightway thou shalt long to eat of them, and the moment thou tastest thereof thou shalt burst. And if any of thy huntsmen hears this thing, and tells thee of it, he shall become stone up to the knee.'" When the huntsman had spoken so far, the horse on which he sat became stone up to the knee. Then he went on, "About the second cockcrow something else came to the window and said the selfsame thing, and prophesied, 'He shall come upon a spring by the roadside, a spring of pure water, and he shall long to drink thereof, and the moment he tastes of it he shall burst; and whoever hears and tells him of this thing shall become stone right up to the girdle.'" And when the huntsman had spoken so far, the horse on which he sat became stone right up to the breast. And he continued, and said, "About the third cockcrow something else came to the window and said the selfsame thing, and added, 'This shall befall thy lord on his way home. He shall come upon a white bed on the road, and he shall desire to rest upon it, and the moment he rests upon it he shall burst; and whoever hears and tells him of this thing shall become stone right up to the neck!'" And with these words he leaped from the horse, and the horse became stone right up to its neck. "That therefore, my master, was why I did what I did, and I pray thee pardon me."

THE STORY OF LITTLE TSAR NOVISHNY, THE FALSE SISTER, AND THE FAITHFUL BEASTS

ONCE upon a time, in a certain kingdom, in a certain empire, there dwelt a certain Tsar who had never had a child. One day this Tsar went to the bazaar (such a bazaar as we have at Kherson) to buy food for his needs. For though he was a Tsar, he had a mean and churlish soul, and used always to do his own marketing, and so now, too, he bought a little salt fish and went home with it. On his way homeward, a great thirst suddenly fell upon him, so he turned aside into a lonely mountain where he knew, as his father had known before him, there was a spring of crystal-clear water. He was so very thirsty that he flung himself down headlong by this spring without first crossing himself, wherefore that Accursed One, Satan, immediately had power over him, and caught him by the beard. The Tsar sprang back in terror, and cried, "Let me go!" But the Accursed One held him all the tighter. "Nay, I will not let thee go!" cried he. Then the Tsar began to entreat him piteously. "Ask what thou wilt of me," said he, "only let me go."--"Give me, then," said the Accursed One, "something that thou hast in the house, and then I'll let thee go!"--"Let me see, what have I got?" said the Tsar. "Oh, I know. I've got eight horses at home, the like of which I have seen nowhere else, and I'll immediately bid my equerry bring them to thee to this spring--take them."--"I *won't* have them!" cried the Accursed One, and he held him still more tightly by the beard. "Well, then, hearken now!" cried the Tsar. "I have eight oxen. They have never yet gone a-ploughing for me, or done a day's work. I'll have them brought hither. I'll feast my eyes on them

33

once more, and then I'll have them driven into thy steppes--take them."--"No, that won't do either!" said the Accursed One. The Tsar went over, one by one, all the most precious things he had at home, but the Accursed One said "No!" all along, and pulled him more and more tightly by the beard. When the Tsar saw that the Accursed One would take none of all these things, he said to him at last, "Look now! I have a wife so lovely that the like of her is not to be found in the whole world, take her and let me go!"-- "No!" replied the Accursed One, "I will not have her." The Tsar was in great straits. "What am I to do now?" thought he. "I have offered him my lovely wife, who is the very choicest of my chattels, and he won't have her!"--Then said the Accursed One, "Promise me what thou shalt find awaiting thee at home, and I'll let thee go."

The Tsar gladly promised this, for he could think of naught else that he had, and then the Accursed One let him go.

But while he had been away from home, there had been born to him a Tsarevko[8] and a Tsarivna; and they grew up not by the day, or even by the hour, but by the minute: never were known such fine children. And his wife saw him coming from afar, and went out to meet him, with her two children, with great joy. But he, the moment he saw them, burst into tears. "Nay, my dear love," cried she, "wherefore dost thou burst into tears? Or art thou so delighted that such children have been born unto thee that thou canst not find thy voice for tears of joy?"--And he answered her, "My darling wife, on my way back from the bazaar I was athirst, and turned toward a mountain known of old to my father and me, and it seemed to me as though there were a spring of water there, though the water was very near dried up. But looking closer, I saw that it was quite full; so I bethought me that I would drink thereof, and I leaned over, when lo! that Evil-wanton (I mean the Devil) caught me by the beard and would not let me go. I begged and prayed, but still he held me tight. 'Give me,' said he, 'what thou hast at home, or I'll never let thee go!'--And I said to him, 'Lo! now, I have horses.'--'I don't want thy horses!' said he.--'I have oxen,' I said.--'I don't want thine oxen!' said he.--'I have,' said I, 'a wife so fair that the like of her is not to be found in God's fair world; take her, but let me go.'--'I don't want thy fair wife!' said he.--Then I promised him what I should find at home when I got there, for I never thought that God had blessed me so. Come now, my darling wife! and let us bury them both lest he take them!"--"Nay, nay! my dear husband, we had better hide them somewhere. Let us dig a ditch by our hut--just under the gables!" (For there were no lordly mansions in those days, and the Tsars dwelt in peasants' huts.) So they dug a ditch right under the gables, and put their children inside it, and gave them provision of bread and water. Then they covered it up and smoothed it down, and turned into their own little hut.

Presently the serpent (for the Accursed One had changed himself into a serpent) came flying up in search of the children. He raged up and down outside the hut--but there was nothing to be seen. At last he cried out to the stove, "Stove, stove, where has the Tsar hidden his children?"--The stove replied, "The Tsar has been a good master to me; he has put lots of warm fuel inside me; I hold to him."--So, finding he could get nothing out of the stove, he cried to the hearth-broom, "Hearth-broom, hearth-broom, where has the Tsar hidden his children?"--But the hearth-broom answered, "The Tsar has always been a good master to me, for he always cleans the warm grate with me; I hold to him." So the Accursed One could get nothing out of the hearth-broom.--Then he cried to the hatchet, "Hatchet, hatchet, where has the Tsar hidden his children?"--The hatchet replied, "The Tsar has always been a good master to me. He chops his wood with me, and gives me a place to lie down in; so I'll not have him disturbed."--Then the Devil cried to the gimlet, "Gimlet, gimlet, where has the Tsar hidden his children?"--But the gimlet replied, "The Tsar has always been a good master to me. He drills little holes with me, and then lets me rest; so I'll let him rest too."--Then the serpent said to the gimlet, "So the Tsar's a good master to thee, eh! Well, I can only say that if he's the good master thou sayest he is, I am

35

rather surprised that he knocks thee on the head so much with a hammer."--"Well, that's true," said the gimlet, "I never thought of that. Thou mayst take hold of me if thou wilt, and draw me out of the top of the hut, near the front gable; and wherever I fall into the marshy ground, there set to work and dig with me!"

The Devil did so, and began digging at the spot where the gimlet fell out on the marshy ground till he had dug out the children. Now, as they had been growing all along, they were children no more, but a stately youth and a fair damsel; and the serpent took them up and carried them off. But they were big and heavy, so he soon got tired and lay down to rest, and presently fell asleep. Then the Tsarivna sat down on his head, and the Tsarevko sat down beside her, till a horse came running up. The horse ran right up to them and said, "Hail! little Tsar Novishny; art thou here by thy leave or against thy leave?"--And the little Tsar Novishny replied, "Nay, little nag! we are here against our leave, not by our leave."--"Then sit on my back!" said the horse, "and I'll carry you off!" So they got on his back, for the serpent was asleep all the time. Then the horse galloped off with them; and he galloped far, far away. Presently the serpent awoke, looked all round him, and could see nothing till he had got up out of the reeds in which he lay, when he saw them in the far distance, and gave chase. He soon caught them up; and little Tsar Novishny said to the horse, "Oh! little nag, how hot it is. It is all up with thee and us!" And, in truth, the horse's tail was already singed to a coal, for the serpent was hard behind them, blazing like fire. The horse perceived that he could do no more, so he gave one last wriggle and died; but they, poor things, were left alive. "Whom have you been listening to?" said the serpent as he flew up to them. "Don't you know that I only am your father and tsar, and have the right to carry you away?"--"Oh, dear daddy! we'll never listen to anybody else again!"--"Well, I'll forgive you this time," said the serpent; "but mind you never do it again."

Again the serpent took them up and carried them off. Presently he grew tired and again lay down to rest, and nodded off. Then the

Tsarivna sat down on his head, and the Tsarevko sat down beside her, till a humble-bee came flying up. "Hail, little Tsar Novishny!" cried the humble-bee.--"Hail, little humble-bee!" said the little Tsar.--"Say, friends, are you here by your leave or against your leave?"--"Alas! little humble-bumble-bee, 'tis not with my leave I have been brought hither, but against my leave, as thou mayst see for thyself."--"Then sit on my back," said the bee, "and I'll carry you away."--"But, dear little humble-bumble-bee, if a horse couldn't save us, how will you?"--"I cannot tell till I try," said the humble-bee. "But if I cannot save you, I'll let you fall."--"Well, then," said the little Tsar, "we'll try. For we two must perish in any case, but thou perhaps mayst get off scot-free." So they embraced each other, sat on the humble-bee, and off they went. When the serpent awoke he missed them, and raising his head above the reeds and rushes, saw them flying far away, and set off after them at full speed. "Alas! little humble-bumble-bee," cried little Tsar Novishny, "how burning hot 'tis getting. We shall all three perish!" Then the humble-bee turned his wing and shook them off. They fell to the earth, and he flew away. Then the serpent came flying up and fell upon them with open jaws. "Ah-ha!" cried he, with a snort, "you've come to grief again, eh? Didn't I tell you to listen to nobody but me!" Then they fell to weeping and entreating, "We'll listen to you alone and to nobody else!" and they wept and entreated so much that at last he forgave them.

So he took them up and carried them off once more. Again he sat down to rest and fell asleep, and again the Tsarivna sat upon his head and the Tsarevko sat down by her side, till a bullock came up, full tilt, and said to them, "Hail, little Tsar Novishny! art thou here with thy leave or art thou here against thy leave?"--"Alas! dear little bullock, I came not hither by my leave; but maybe I was brought here against my leave!"--"Sit on my back, then," said the bullock, "and I'll carry you away."--But they said, "Nay, if a horse and a bee could not manage it, how wilt thou?"-- "Nonsense!" said the bullock. "Sit down, and I'll carry you off!" So he persuaded them.--"Well, we can only perish once!" they cried; and the bullock carried them off. And every little while they went a little mile, and jolted so that they very nearly tumbled off. Presently the serpent awoke and was very very wrath. He rose high above the woods and flew after them--oh! how fast he did fly! Then cried the little Tsar, "Alas! bullock, how hot it turns. Thou wilt perish, and we shall perish also!"--Then said the bullock, "Little Tsar! look into my left ear and thou wilt see a horse-comb. Pull it out and throw it behind thee!"--The little Tsar took out the comb and threw it behind him, and it became a huge wood, as thick and jagged as the teeth of a horse-comb. But the bullock went on at his old pace: every little while they went a little mile, and jolted so that they nearly tumbled off. The serpent, however, managed to gnaw his way through the wood, and then flew after them again. Then cried the little Tsar, "Alas! bullock, it begins to burn again. Thou wilt perish, and we shall perish also!"--Then said the bullock, "Look into my right ear, and pull out the brush thou dost find there, and fling it behind thee!"--So he threw it behind him, and it became a forest as thick as a brush. Then the serpent came up to the forest and began to gnaw at it; and at last he gnawed his way right through it. But the bullock went on at his old pace: every little while they went a little mile, and they jolted so that they nearly tumbled off. But when the serpent had gnawed his way through the forest, he again pursued them; and again they felt a burning. And the little Tsar said, "Alas! bullock, look! look! how it burns. Look! look! how we perish." Now the bullock was already nearing the sea. "Look into my right ear," said the bullock, "draw out the little handkerchief thou findest there, and throw it in front of me." He drew it out and flung it, and before them stood a bridge. Over this bridge they galloped, and by the time they had done so, the serpent reached the sea. Then said the bullock to the little Tsar, "Take up the handkerchief again and wave it behind me." Then he took and waved it till the bridge doubled up behind them, and went and spread out again right in front of them. The serpent came up to the edge of the sea; but there he had to stop, for he had nothing to run upon.

So they crossed over that sea right to the other side, and the serpent remained on his own side. Then the bullock said to them, "I'll lead you to a hut close to the sea, and in that hut you must live, and you must take and slay me." But they fell a-weeping sore. "How shall we slay thee!" they cried; "thou art our own little dad, and hast saved us from death!"--"Nay!" said the bullock; "but you must slay me, and one quarter of me you must hang up on the stove, and the second quarter you must place on the ground in a corner, and the third quarter you must put in the corner at the entrance of the hut, and the fourth quarter you must put round the threshold, so that there will be a quarter in all four corners." So they took and slew him in front of the threshold, and they hung his four quarters in the four corners as he had bidden them, and then they laid them down to sleep. Now the Tsarevko awoke at midnight, and saw in the right-hand corner a horse so gorgeously caparisoned that he could not resist rising at once and mounting it; and in the threshold corner there was a self-slicing sword, and in the third corner stood the dog *Protius*[9], and in the stove corner stood the dog *Nedviga*[9]. The little Tsar longed to be off. "Rise, little sister!" cried he. "God has been good to us! Rise, dear little sister, and let us pray to God!" So they arose and prayed to God, and while they prayed the day dawned. Then he mounted his horse and took the dogs with him, that he might live by what they caught.

So they lived in their hut by the sea, and one day the sister went down to the sea to wash her bed-linen and her body-linen in the blue waters. And the serpent came and said to her, "How didst thou manage to jump over the sea?"--"Look, now!" said she, "we crossed over in this way. My brother has a handkerchief which becomes a bridge when he waves it behind him."--And the serpent said to her, "I tell thee what, ask him for this handkerchief; say thou dost want to wash it, and take and wave it, and I'll then be able to cross over to thee and live with thee, and we'll poison thy brother."--Then she went home and said to her brother, "Give me that handkerchief, dear little brother; it is dirty, so I'll wash and give it back to thee." And he believed her and gave it to her, for she was dear to him, and he thought her good and true. Then she took the handkerchief, went down to the sea, and waved it--and behold there was a bridge. Then the serpent crossed over to her side, and they walked to the hut together and consulted as to the best way of destroying her brother and removing him from God's fair world. Now it was his custom to rise at dawn, mount his horse, and go a-hunting, for hunting he dearly loved. So the serpent said to her, "Take to thy bed and pretend to be ill, and say to him, 'I dreamed a dream, dear brother, and lo, I saw thee go and fetch me wolf's milk to make me well.' Then he'll go and fetch it, and the wolves will tear his dogs to pieces, and then we can take and do to him as we list, for his strength is in his dogs."

So when the brother came home from hunting the serpent hid himself, but the sister said, "I have dreamed a dream, dear brother. Methought thou didst go and fetch me wolf's milk, and I drank of it, and my health came back to me, for I am so weak that God grant I die not."--"I'll fetch it," said her brother. So he mounted his horse and set off. Presently he came to a little thicket, and immediately a she-wolf came out. Then Protius ran her down and Nedviga held her fast, and the little Tsar milked her and let her go. And the she-wolf looked round and said, "Well for thee, little Tsar Novishny, that thou hast let me go. Methought thou wouldst not let me go alive. For that thou hast let me go, I'll give thee, little Tsar Novishny, a wolf-whelp."--Then she said to the little wolf, "Thou shalt serve this dear little Tsar as though he were thine own dear father." Then the little Tsar went back, and now there were with him two dogs and a little wolf-whelp that trotted behind them.

Now the serpent and the false sister saw him coming from afar, and three dogs trotting behind him. And the serpent said to her, "What a sly, wily one it is! He has added another watch-dog to his train! Lie down, and make thyself out worse than ever, and ask bear's milk of him, for the bears will tear him to pieces without doubt." Then the serpent turned himself into a needle, and she took him up and stuck him in the wall. Meanwhile the brother dismounted from his horse and came with his dogs and the wolf to the hut, and the dogs began snuffing at the needle in the wall. And his sister said to him, "Tell me, why dost thou keep these big dogs? They let me have no rest." Then he called to the dogs, and they sat down. And his sister said to him, "I dreamed a dream, my brother. I saw thee go and search and fetch me from somewhere bear's milk, and I drank of it, and my health came back to me."--"I will fetch it," said her brother.

But first of all he laid him down to sleep. Nedviga lay at his head, and Protius at his feet, and *Vovchok*[10] by his side. So he slept through the night, and at dawn he arose and mounted his good steed and hied him thence. Again they came to a little thicket, and this time a she-bear came out. Protius ran her down, Nedviga held her fast, and the little Tsar milked her and let her go. Then the she-bear said, "Hail to thee, little Tsar Novishny; because thou hast let me go, I'll give thee a bear-cub." But to the little bear she said, "Obey him as though he were thine own father." So he set off home, and the serpent and his sister saw that four were now trotting behind him. "Look!" said the serpent, "if there are not four running behind him! Shall we never be able to destroy him? I tell thee what. Ask him to get thee hare's milk; perhaps his beasts will gobble up the hare before he can milk it." So he turned himself into a needle again, and she fastened him in the wall, only a little higher up, so that the dogs should not get at him. Then, when the little Tsar dismounted from his horse, he and his dogs came into the hut, and the dogs began snuffing at the needle in the wall and barked at it, but the brother knew not the cause thereof. But his sister burst into tears and said, "Why dost thou keep such monstrous dogs? Such a kennel of them makes me ill with anguish!" Then he shouted to the dogs, and they sat down quite still. Then she said to him, "I am so ill, brother, that nothing will make me well but hare's milk. Go and get it for me."--"I'll get it," said he.

But first he laid him down to sleep. Nedviga lay at his head, Protius at his feet, and Vovchok and *Medvedik*[11] each on one side. He slept through the night, but at dawn he mounted his steed, took his pack with him, and departed. Again he came to a little thicket, and a she-hare popped out. Protius ran her down, Nedviga held her fast, then he milked her and let her go. Then the hare said, "Hail to thee, little Tsar Novishny; because thou hast let me go--I thought thou wouldst have torn me to pieces with thy dogs--I'll give thee a leveret." But to the leveret she said, "Obey him, as though he were thine own father." Then he went home, and again they saw him from afar. "What a wily rogue it is!" said they. "All five are following him, and he is as well as ever!"--"Ask him to get thee fox's milk!" said the serpent; "perhaps when he goes for it his beasts will leave him in the lurch!" Then he changed himself into a needle, and she stuck him still higher in the wall, so that the dogs could not get at him. The Tsar again dismounted from his horse, and his dogs rushed up to the hut and began snuffing at the needle. But his sister fell a-weeping, and said, "Why dost thou keep such monstrous dogs?" He shouted to them, and they sat down quietly on their haunches. Then his sister said again, "I am ailing, my brother; go and get me fox's milk, and I shall be well."--"I'll fetch it for thee," said her brother.

But first he lay down to sleep. Nedviga lay at his head, Protius at his feet, and Vovchok, Medvedik, and the leveret by his side. The little Tsar slept through the night, and at dawn he arose, mounted his horse, took his pack with him, and went off. They came to a little thicket, and a vixen popped out. Protius ran her down, Nedviga held her fast, and the little Tsar milked her and let her go. Then said the vixen to him, "Thanks to thee, little Tsar Novishny, that thou hast let me go. Methought thou wouldst tear me in pieces with thy dogs. For thy kindness I'll give thee a little fox." But to the little fox she said, "Obey him as though he were thine own father." So he went home, and they saw him coming from afar, and lo! now he had six guardians, and yet had come by no harm. "'Tis no good; we shall never do for him," said the serpent. "Look, now! Make thyself worse than ever, and say to him, 'I am very ill, my brother, because in another realm, far, far away, there is a wild boar who ploughs with his nose, and sows with his ears, and harrows with his tail--and in that same empire there is a mill with twelve furnaces that grinds its own grain and casts forth its own meal, and if thou wilt bring me of the meal that is beneath these twelve furnaces, so that I may make me a cake of it and eat, my soul shall live.'"--Then her brother said to her, "Methinks thou art not my sister, but my foe!"--But she replied, "How can I be thy foe when we two live all alone together in a strange land?"--"Well, I will get it for thee," said he. For again he believed in his sister.

So he mounted his steed, took his pack with him, and departed, and he came to the land where were that boar and that mill she had told him of. He came up to the mill, tied his horse to it, and entered into it. And there were twelve furnaces there and twelve doors, and these twelve doors needed no man to open or shut them, for they opened and shut themselves. He took meal from beneath the first furnace and went through the second door, but the dogs were shut in by the doors. Through all twelve doors he went, and came out again at the first door, and looked about him, and--there were no dogs to be seen. He whistled, and he heard his dogs whining where they could not get out. Then he wept sore, mounted his horse, and went home. He got home, and there was his sister making merry with the serpent. And no sooner did the brother enter the hut than the serpent said, "Well, we wanted flesh, and now flesh has come to us!" For they had just slain a bullock, and on the ground where they had slain it there sprang up a whitethorn-tree, so lovely that it may be told of in tales, but neither imagined nor divined. When the little Tsar saw it, he said, "Oh, my dear brother-in-law!" (for without his dogs he must needs be courteous to the serpent) "pray let me climb up that whitethorn-tree, and have a good look about me!" But the sister said to the serpent, "Dear friend, make him get ready boiling water for himself, and we will boil him, for it does not become

43

thee to dirty thy hands."--"Very well," said the serpent; "he shall make the boiling water ready!" So they ordered the little Tsar to go and chop wood and get the hot water ready. Then he went and chopped wood, but as he was doing so, a starling flew out and said to him, "Not so fast, not so fast, little Tsar Novishny. Be as slow as thou canst, for thy dogs have gnawed their way through two doors."

Then the little Tsar poured water into the cauldron, and put fire under it. But the wood that he had cut was rotten and very very dry, so that it burned most fiercely, and he took and sprinkled it with water, and sprinkled it again and again, so that it might not burn too much. And when he went out into the courtyard for more water, the starling said to him, "Not so fast, not so fast, little Tsar Novishny, for thy dogs have gnawed their way through four doors!" As he was returning to the hut his sister said to him, "That water does not boil up quickly enough! Take the fire-shovel and poke the fire!" So he did so, and the faggots blazed up, but when she had gone away he sprinkled them with water again, so that they might burn more slowly. Then he went into the courtyard again, and the starling met him and said, "Not so fast, not so fast, little Tsar; be as slow as thou canst, for thy dogs have gnawed their way through six doors." Then he returned to the hut, and his sister again took up the shovel and made him poke up the fire, and when she went away he again flung water on the burning coals. So he kept going in and out of the courtyard. "'Tis weary work!" cried he; but the starling said to him, "Not so fast, not so fast, little Tsar Novishny, for thy dogs have already gnawed their way through ten doors!" The little Tsar picked up the rottenest wood he could find and flung it on the fire, to make believe he was making haste, but sprinkled it at the same time with water, so that it might not burn up too quickly, and yet the kettle soon began to boil. Again he went to the forest for more wood, and the starling said to him, "Not so fast, not so fast, little Tsar, for thy dogs have already gnawed their way through all the doors, and are now resting!" But now the water was boiling, and his sister ran up and said to him, "Come, boil thyself, be quick; how much longer art thou going to keep us waiting?" Then he, poor thing, began ladling the boiling water over himself, while she got the table ready and spread the cloth, that the serpent might eat her brother on that very table.

But he, poor thing, kept ladling himself, and cried, "Oh, my dear brother-in-law, pray let me climb up to the top of that whitethorn-tree; let me have a look out from the top of it, for thence one can see afar!"--"Don't let him, dear!" said the sister to the serpent; "he will stay there too long and lose our precious time."--But the serpent replied, "It doesn't matter, it doesn't matter; let him climb up if he likes." So the little Tsar went up to the tree, and began to climb it; he did not miss a single branch, and stopped a little at each one to gain time, and so he climbed up to the very top, and then he took out his flute and began to play upon it. But the starling flew up to him and said, "Not so fast, little Tsar Novishny, for lo! thy dogs are running to thee with all their might." But his sister ran out and said, "What art thou playing up there for? Thou dost forget perhaps that we are waiting for thee down here!" Then he began to descend the tree, but he stopped at every branch on his way down, while his sister kept on calling to him to come down quicker. At last he came to the last branch, and as he stood upon it and leaped down to the ground, he thought to himself, "Now I perish!" At that same instant his dogs and his beasts, growling loudly, came running up, and stood in a circle around him. Then he crossed himself and said, "Glory to Thee, O Lord! I have still, perchance, a little time to live in Thy fair world!" Then he called aloud to the serpent and said, "And now, dear brother-in-law, come out, for I am ready for thee!" Out came the serpent to eat him, but he said to his dogs and his beasts, "Vovchok! Medvedik! Protius! Nedviga! Seize him!" Then the dogs and the beasts rushed upon him and tore him to bits.

Then the little Tsar collected the pieces and burnt them to ashes, and the little fox rolled his brush in the ashes till it was covered with them, and then went out into the open field and scattered

45

them to the four winds. But while they were tearing the serpent to pieces the wicked sister knocked out his tooth and hid it. After it was all over the little Tsar said to her, "As thou hast been such a false friend to me, sister, thou must remain here while I go into another kingdom." Then he made two buckets and hung them up on the whitethorn-tree, and said to his sister, "Look now, sister! if thou weepest for me, this bucket will fill with tears, but if thou weepest for the serpent that bucket will fill with blood!" Then she fell a-weeping and praying, and said to him, "Don't leave me, brother, but take me with thee."--"I won't," said he; "such a false friend as thou art I'll not have with me. Stay where thou art." So he mounted his horse, called to him his dogs and his beasts, and went his way into another kingdom and into another empire.

He went on and on till he came to a certain city, and in this city there was only one spring, and in this spring sat a dragon with twelve heads. And it was so that when any went to draw water from this well the dragon rose up and ate them, and there was no other place whence that city could draw its water. So the little Tsar came to that town and put up at the stranger's inn, and he asked his host, "What is the meaning of all this running and crying of the people in the streets?"--"Why, dost thou not know?" said he; "it is the turn of the Tsar to send his daughter to the dragon!"--Then he went out and listened, and heard the people say, "The Tsar proclaims that whoever is able to slay the dragon, to him will he give his daughter and one-half of his tsardom!" Then little Tsar Novishny stepped forth and said, "I am able to slay this evil dragon!" So all the people immediately sent and told the Tsar, "A stranger has come hither who says he is ready to meet and slay the dragon." Then the Tsar bade them take him to the watch-house and put him among the guards.

Then they led out the Tsarivna, and behind her they led him, and behind him came his beasts and his horse. And the Tsarivna was so lovely and so richly attired that all who beheld her burst into tears. But the moment the dragon appeared and opened his mouth to devour the Tsarivna, the little Tsar cried to his self-slicing sword, "Fall upon him!" and to his beasts he cried, "Protius! Medvedik! Vovchok! Nedviga! Seize him!" Then the self-slicing sword and the beasts fell upon him, and tore him into little bits. When they had finished tearing him, the little Tsar took the remains of the body and burnt them to ashes, and the little fox took up all the ashes on her tail, and scattered them to the four winds. Then he took the Tsarivna by the hand, and led her to the Tsar, and the people rejoiced because their water was free again. And the Tsarivna gave him the nuptial ring.

Then they set off home again. They went on and on, for it was a long way from the tsardom of that Tsar, and at last he grew weary and lay down in the grass, and she sat at his head. Then his lackey crept up to him, unfastened the self-slicing sword from his side, went up to the little Tsar, and said, "Self-slicing sword! slay him!" Then the self-slicing sword cut him into little bits, and his beasts knew nothing about it, for they were sleeping after their labours. After that the lackey said to the Tsarivna, "Thou must say now to all men that I saved thee from death, or if not, I will do to thee what I have done to him. Swear that thou wilt say this thing!" Then she said, "I will swear that thou didst save me from death," for she was sore afraid of the lackey. Then they returned to the city, and the Tsar was very glad to see them, and clothed the lackey in goodly apparel, and they all made merry together.

Now when Nedviga awoke he perceived that his master was no longer there, and immediately awoke all the rest, and they all began to think and consider which of them was the swiftest. And when they had thought it well over they judged that the hare was the swiftest, and they resolved that the hare should run and get living and healing water and the apple of youth also. So the hare ran to fetch this water and this apple, and he ran and ran till he came to a certain land, and in this land the hare saw a spring, and close to the spring grew an apple-tree with the apples of youth, and this spring and this apple-tree were guarded by a Muscovite, oh! so strong, so strong, and he waved his sabre again and again so that not even a mouse could make its way up to that well.

What was to be done? Then the little hare had resort to subtlety, and made herself crooked, and limped toward the spring as if she were lame. When the Muscovite saw her he said, "What sort of a little beast is this? I never saw the like of it before!" So the hare passed him by, and went farther and farther on till she came right up to the well. The Muscovite stood there and opened his eyes wide, but the hare had now got up to the spring, and took a little flask of the water and nipped off a little apple, and was off in a trice.

She ran back to the little Tsar Novishny, and Nedviga immediately took the water and sprinkled therewith the fragments of the little Tsar, and the fragments came together again. Then he poured some of the living water into his mouth and he became alive, and gave him a bite of the apple of youth, and he instantly grew young again and stronger than ever. Then the little Tsar rose upon his feet, stretched himself, and yawned. "What a long time I've been asleep!" cried he.--"'Tis a good thing for thee that we got the living and healing water!" said Protius.-- "But what shall we do next?" said they all. Then they all took council together, and agreed that the little Tsar should disguise himself as an old man, and so go to the Tsar's palace.

So the little Tsar Novishny disguised himself as an old man, and went to the palace of the Tsar. And when he got there he begged them to let him in that he might see the young married people. But the lackeys would not let him in. Then the Tsarivna herself heard the sound of his begging and praying, and commanded them to admit him. Now when he entered the room and took off his cap and cloak, the ring which the Tsarivna had given him when he slew the serpent sparkled so that she knew him, but, not believing her own eyes, she said to him, "Come hither, thou godly old pilgrim, that I may show thee hospitality!" Then the little Tsar drew near to the table, and the Tsarivna poured him out a glass of wine and gave it to him, and he took it with his left hand. She marked that he did not take it with the hand on which was the ring, so she drank off that glass herself. Then she filled another glass and gave it him, and he took it with his right hand. Then she immediately recognized her ring, and said to her father, "This man is my husband who delivered me from death, but that fellow"--pointing to the lackey--"that rascally slavish soul killed my husband and made me say that he was my husband." When the Tsar heard this he boiled over with rage. "So *that* is what thou art!" said he to the lackey, and immediately he bade them bind him and tie him to the tail of a horse so savage that no man could ride it, and then turn it loose into the endless steppe. But the little Tsar Novishny sat down behind the table and made merry.

So the Tsarevko and the Tsarivna lived a long time together in happiness, but one day she asked him, "What of thy kindred and thy father's house?" Then he told her all about his sister. She immediately bade him saddle his horse, and taking his beasts with him, go in search of her. They came to the place where he had left her, and saw that the bucket which was put up for the serpent was full of blood, but that the little Tsar's bucket was all dry and falling to pieces. Then he perceived that she was still lamenting for the serpent, and said to her, "God be with thee, but I will know thee no more. Stay here, and never will I look upon thy face again!" But she began to entreat and caress and implore him that he would take her with him. Then the brother had compassion on his sister and took her away with him.

Now when they got home she took out the serpent's tooth which she had hidden about her, and put it beneath his pillow on the bed whereon he slept. And at night-time the little Tsar went to lie down and the tooth killed him. His wife thought that he was sulky, and therefore did not speak to her, so she begged him not to be angry; and, getting no answer, took him by the hand, and lo! his hand was cold, as cold as lead, and she screamed out. But Protius came bounding through the door and kissed his master. Then the little Tsar became alive again, but Protius died. Then Nedviga kissed Protius and Protius became alive, but Nedviga died. Then the Tsarevko said to Medvedik, "Kiss Nedviga!" He did so, and Nedviga became alive again, but Medvedik died. And so they went on kissing each other from the greatest to the smallest, till the turn came to the hare. She kissed Vovchok and died, but Vovchok remained alive. What was to be done? Now that the little hare had died there was none to kiss her back into life again. "Kiss her," said the little Tsar to the little fox. But the little fox was artful, and taking the little hare on his shoulder, he trotted off to the forest. He carried her to a place where lay a felled oak, with two branches one on the top of the other, and put the hare on the lower branch; then he ran under the branch and kissed the hare, but took good care that the branch should be between them. Thereupon the serpent's tooth flew out of the hare and fastened itself in the upper branch, and both fox and hare scampered back out of the forest alive and well. When the others saw them both alive they rejoiced greatly that no harm had come to any of them from the tooth. But they seized the sister and tied her to the tail of a savage horse and let her loose upon the endless steppe.

So they all lived the merry lives of Tsars who feast continually. And I was there too, and drank wine and mead till my mouth ran over and it trickled all down my beard. So there's the whole *kazka* for you.

THE VAMPIRE AND ST MICHAEL

ONCE upon a time in a certain village there lived two neighbours; one was rich, very rich, and the other so poor that he had nothing in the world but a little hut, and that was tumbling about his ears. At length things came to such a pass with the poor man that he had nothing to eat, and could get work nowhere. Full of grief, he bethought him what he should do. He thought and thought, and at last he said, "Look ye, wife! I'll go to my rich neighbour. Perchance he will lend me a silver rouble; that, at any rate, will be enough to buy bread with." So he went.

He came to the rich man. "Good health to my lord!" cried he.-- "Good health!"--"I have come on an errand to thee, dear little master!"--"What may thine errand be?" inquired the rich man.-- "Alas! would to God that I had no need to say it. It has come to such a pass with us that there's not a crust of bread nor a farthing of money in the house. So I have come to thee, dear little master; lend us but a silver rouble and we will be ever thankful to thee, and I'll work myself old to pay it back."--"But who will stand surety for thee?" asked the rich man.--"I know not if any man will, I am so poor. Yet, perchance, God and St Michael will be my sureties," and he pointed at the ikon in the corner. Then the ikon of St Michael spoke to the rich man from the niche and said, "Come now! lend it him, and put it down to my account. God will repay thee!"--"Well," said the rich man, "I'll lend it to thee." So he lent it, and the poor man thanked him and returned to his home full of joy.

But the rich man was not content that God should give him back his loan by blessing him in his flocks and herds, and in his children, and in his health, and in the blessed fruits of the earth.

51

He waited and waited for the poor man to come and pay him back his rouble, and at last he went to seek him. "Thou son of a dog," he shouted, before the house, "why hast thou not brought me back my money? Thou knowest how to borrow, but thou forgettest to repay!" Then the wife of the poor man burst into tears. "He would repay thee indeed if he were in this world," said she, "but lo now! he died but a little while ago!" The rich man snarled at her and departed, but when he got home he said to the ikon, "A pretty surety *thou* art!" Then he took St Michael down from the niche, dug out his eyes, and began beating him.

He beat St Michael again and again, and at last he flung him into a puddle and trampled on him. "I'll give it thee for standing me surety so scurvily," said he. While he was thus abusing St Michael, a young fellow about twenty years old came along that way, and said to him, "What art thou doing, my father?"--"I am beating him because he stood surety and has played me false. He took upon himself the repayment of a silver rouble, which I lent to the son of a pig, who has since gone away and died. That is why I am beating him now."--"Beat him not, my father! I'll give thee a silver rouble, but do thou give me this holy image!"--"Take him if thou wilt, but see that thou bring me the silver rouble first."

Then the young man ran home and said to his father, "Dad, give me a silver rouble!"--"Wherefore, my son?"--"I would buy a holy image," said he, and he told his father how he had seen that heathen beating St Michael.--"Nay, my son, whence shall we who are poor find a silver rouble to give to him who is so rich?"--"Nay, but give it me, dad!" and he begged and prayed till he got it. Then he ran back as quickly as he could, paid the silver rouble to the rich man, and got the holy image. He washed it clean and placed it in the midst of sweet-smelling flowers. And so they lived on as before.

Now this youth had three uncles, rich merchants, who sold all manner of merchandise, and went in ships to foreign lands, where they sold their goods and made their gains. One day, when his uncles were again making ready to depart into foreign lands, he said to them, "Take me with you!"--"Why shouldst thou go?" said they; "we have wares to sell, but what hast thou?"--"Yet take me," said he.--"But thou hast nothing."--"I will make me laths and boards and take them with me," said he.--His uncles laughed at him for imagining such wares as these, but he begged and prayed them till they were wearied. "Well, come," they said, "though there is naught for thee to do; only take not much of these wares of thine with thee, for our ships are already full."-- Then he made him laths and boards, put them on board the ship, took St Michael with him, and they departed.

They went on and on. They sailed a short distance and they sailed a long distance, till at last they came to another tsardom and another empire. And the Tsar of this tsardom had an only daughter, so lovely that the like of her is neither to be imagined nor divined in God's fair world, neither may it be told in tales. Now this Tsarivna one day went down to the river to bathe, and plunged into the water without first crossing herself, whereupon the Evil Spirit took possession of her. The Tsarivna got out of the water, and straightway fell ill of so terrible a disease that it may not be told of. Do what they would--and the wise men and the wise women did their utmost--it was of no avail. In a few days she grew worse and died. Then the Tsar, her father, made a proclamation that people should come and read the prayers for the dead over her dead body, and so exorcise the evil spirit, and whosoever delivered her was to have half his power and half his tsardom.

And the people came in crowds--but none of them could read the prayers for the dead over her, it was impossible. Every evening a man went into the church, and every morning they swept out his bones, for there was naught else of him remaining. And the Tsar was very wrath. "All my people will be devoured," cried he. And he commanded that all the foreign merchants passing through his realm should be made to read prayers for the dead over his

THE TSARIVNA AROSE FROM HER COFFIN

daughter's body. "And if they will not read," said he, "they shall not depart from my kingdom."

So the foreign merchants went one by one. In the evening a merchant was shut up in the church, and in the early morning they came and found and swept away his bones. At last it came to the turn of the young man's uncles to read the prayers for the dead in the church. They wept and lamented and cried, "We are lost! we are lost! Heaven help us!" Then the eldest uncle said to the lad, "Listen, good simpleton! It has now come to my turn to read prayers over the Tsarivna. Do thou go in my stead and pass the night in the church, and I'll give thee all my ship."--"Nay, but," said the simpleton, "what if she tear me to pieces too? I won't go!"--But then St Michael said to him, "Go and fear not! Stand in the very middle of the church, fenced round about with thy laths and boards, and take with thee a basket full of pears. When she rushes at thee, take and scatter the pears, and it will take her till cockcrow to pick them all up. But do thou go on reading thy prayers all the time, and look not up, whatever she may do."

When night came, he took up his laths and boards and a basket of pears, and went to the church. He entrenched himself behind his boards, stood there and began to read. At dead of night there was a rustling and a rattling. O Lord! what was that? There was a shaking of the bier--bang! bang!--and the Tsarivna arose from her coffin and came straight toward him. She leaped upon the boards and made a grab at him and fell back. Then she leaped at him again, and again she fell back. Then he took his basket and scattered the pears. All through the church they rolled, she after them, and she tried to pick them up till cockcrow, and at the very first "Cock-a-doodle-doo!" she got into her bier again and lay still.

When God's bright day dawned, the people came to clean out the church and sweep away his bones; but there he was reading his prayers, and the rumour of it went through the town and they were all filled with joy.

Next night it was the turn of the second uncle, and he began to beg and pray, "Go thou, simpleton, in my stead! Look now, thou hast already passed a night there, thou mayst very well pass another, and I'll give thee all my ship."--But he said, "I won't go, I am afraid."--But then St Michael said to him again, "Fear not, but go! Fence thee all about with thy boards, and take with thee a basket of nuts. When she rushes at thee, scatter thy nuts, and the nuts will go rolling all about the church, and it will take her till cockcrow to gather them all up. But do thou go on reading thy prayers, nor look thou up, whatever may happen."

And he did so. He took his boards and the basket of nuts, and went to the church at nightfall and read. A little after midnight there was a rustling and an uproar, and the whole church shook. Then came a fumbling round about the coffin--bang! bang!--up she started, and made straight for him. She leaped and plunged, she very nearly got through the boards. She hissed, like seething pitch, and her eyes glared at him like coals of fire, but it was of no use. He read on and on, and didn't once look at her. Besides, he scattered his nuts, and she went after them and tried to pick them all up till cockcrow. And at the first "Cock-a-doodle-doo!" she leaped into her coffin again and pulled down the lid. In the morning the people came to sweep away his bones, and lo! they found him alive.

The next night he had to go again in the third uncle's stead. Then he sat down and cried and wailed, "Alas, alas! what shall I do? 'Twere better I had never been born!"--But St Michael said to him, "Weep not, 'twill all end happily. Fence thyself about with thy boards, sprinkle thyself all about with holy water, incense thyself with holy incense, and take me with thee. She shall not have thee. And the moment she leaves her coffin, do thou jump quickly into it. And whatever she may say to thee, and however she may implore thee, let her not get into it again until she says to thee, '*My consort!*'"

So he went. There he stood in the middle of the church, fenced himself about with his boards, strewed consecrated poppy-seed around him, incensed himself with holy incense, and read and read. About the middle of the night a tempest arose outside, and there was a rustling and a roaring, a hissing and a wailing. The church shook, the altar candelabra were thrown down, the holy images fell on their faces. O Lord, how awful! Then came a bang! bang! from the coffin, and again the Tsarivna started up. She left her coffin and fluttered about the church. She rushed at the boards and made a snatch at him, and fell back; she rushed at him again, and again she fell back. She foamed at the mouth, and her fury every instant grew worse and worse. She dashed herself about, and darted madly from one corner of the church to the other, seeking him everywhere. But he skipped into the coffin, with the image of St Michael by his side. She ran all over the church seeking him. "He was here--and now he is not here!" cried she. Then she ran farther on, felt all about her, and cried again, "He was here--and now he's not here!" At last she sprang up to the coffin, and there he was. Then she began to beg and pray him, "Come down, come down! I'll try and catch thee no more, only come down, come down!" But he only prayed to God, and answered her never a word. Then the cock crew once, "Cock-a-doodle-doo!"--"Alas! come down, come down, *my consort!*" cried she. Then he came down, and they both fell on their knees and began praying to God, and wept sore and gave thanks to God because He had had mercy on them both.

And at dawn of day crowds of people, with the Tsar at the head of them, came to the church. "Shall we find him reading prayers, or shall we only find his bones?" said they. And lo! there they both were on their knees praying fervently to God. Then the Tsar rejoiced greatly, and embraced both him and her. After that they had a grand service in the church, and sprinkled her with holy water, and baptized her again, and the unclean spirit departed from her. Then the Tsar gave the young man half his power and

THEY WERE BOTH ON THEIR KNEES

half his kingdom, but the merchants departed in their ships, with their nephew on board.

They lived together, and time went on and the young man still remained a bachelor, and was so handsome that words cannot describe it. But the Tsar lived alone with his daughter. She, however, grew sadder and sadder, and was no longer like her former self, so sorrowful was she. And the Tsar asked her, saying, "Wherefore art thou so sorrowful?"--"I am not sorrowful, father," said she. But the Tsar watched her, and saw that she *was* sorrowful, and there was no help for it. Then he asked her again, "Art thou ill?"--"Nay, dear dad," said she. "I myself know not what is the matter with me."

And so it went on, till the Tsar dreamt a dream, and in this dream it was said to him, "Thy daughter grieves because she loves so much the youth who drove the unclean spirit out of her." Then the Tsar asked her, "Dost thou love this youth?"--And she answered, "I do, dear father."--"Then why didst thou not tell me before, my daughter?" said he. Then he sent for his heyducks and commanded them, saying, "Go this instant to such and such a kingdom, and there ye will find the youth who cured my daughter; bring him to me." Then they went on and on until they found him, and he took just the same laths and boards that he had had before, and went with them. The Tsar met him, and bought all his boards, and when they split them in pieces, lo! they were full of precious stones. Then the Tsar took him to his own house and gave him his daughter. And they lived right merrily together.

R. Nisbet Bain

THE STORY OF TREMSIN, THE BIRD ZHAR, AND NASTASIA, THE LOVELY MAID OF THE SEA

THERE was once upon a time a man and a woman, and they had one little boy. In the summertime they used to go out and mow corn in the fields, and one summer when they had laid their little lad by the side of a sheaf, an eagle swooped down, caught up the child, carried him into a forest, and laid him in its nest. Now in this forest three bandits chanced to be wandering at the same time. They heard the child crying in the eagle's nest: "Oo-oo! oo-oo! oo-oo!" so they went up to the oak on which was the nest and said one to another, "Let us hew down the tree and kill the child!"--"No," replied one of them, "it were better to climb up the tree and bring him down alive." So he climbed up the tree and brought down the lad, and they nurtured him and gave him the name of Tremsin. They brought up Tremsin until he became a youth, and then they gave him a horse, set him upon it, and said to him, "Now go out into the wide world and search for thy father and thy mother!" So Tremsin went out into the wide world and pastured his steed on the vast steppes, and his steed spoke to him and said, "When we have gone a little farther, thou wilt see before thee a plume of the Bird *Zhar*[12]; pick it not up, or sore trouble will be thine!" Then they went on again. They went on and on, through ten tsardoms they went, till they came to another empire in the land of Thrice Ten where lay the feather. And the youth said to himself, "Why should I not pick up the feather when it shines so brightly even from afar?" And he went near to the feather, and it shone so that the like of it cannot be expressed or conceived or imagined or even told of in tales. Then Tremsin

61

picked up the feather and went into the town over against him, and in that town there lived a rich nobleman. And Tremsin entered the house of this nobleman and said, "Sir, may I not take service with thee as a labourer?"--The nobleman looked at him, and seeing that he was comely and stalwart, "Why not? Of course thou mayst," said he. So he took him into his service. Now this nobleman had many servants, and they curried his horses for him, and made them smart and glossy against the day he should go a-hunting. And Tremsin began to curry his horse likewise, and the servants of the nobleman could not make the horses of their master so shining bright as Tremsin made his own horse. So they looked more closely, and they perceived that when Tremsin cleaned his horse he stroked it with the feather of the Bird Zhar, and the coat of the good steed straightway shone like burnished silver. Then those servants were filled with envy, and said among themselves, "How can we remove this fellow from the world? We'll saddle him with a task he is unable to do, and then our master will drive him away."--So they went to their master and said, "Tremsin has a feather of the Bird Zhar, and he says that if he likes he can get the Bird Zhar itself." Then the nobleman sent for Tremsin and said to him, "O Tremsin! my henchmen say that thou canst get the Bird Zhar if thou dost choose."--"Nay, but I cannot," replied Tremsin.--"Answer me not," said the nobleman, "for so sure as I've a sword, I'll slice thy head off like a gourd."-- Then Tremsin fell a-weeping and went away to his horse. "My master," said he, "hath given me a task to do that will clean undo me."--"What task is that?" asked the horse.--"Why, to fetch him the Bird Zhar."--"Why that's not a task, but a trifle," replied the horse. "Let us go to the steppes," it continued, "and let me go a-browsing; but do thou strip thyself stark-naked and lie down in the grass, and the Bird Zhar will straightway swoop down to feed. So long as she only claws about thy body, touch her not; but as soon as she begins to claw at thine eyes, seize her by the legs."

So when they got to the wild steppes, Tremsin stripped himself naked and flung himself in the grass, and, immediately, the Bird

Zhar swooped down and began pecking all about him, and at last she pecked at his eyes. Then Tremsin seized her by both legs, and mounted his horse and took the Bird Zhar to the nobleman. Then his fellow-servants were more envious than ever, and they said among themselves, "How shall we devise for him a task to do that cannot be done, and so rid the world of him altogether?" So they bethought them, and then they went to the nobleman and said, "Tremsin says that to get the Bird Zhar was nothing, and that he is also able to get the thrice-lovely Nastasia of the sea." Then the nobleman again sent for Tremsin and said to him, "Look now! thou didst get for me the Bird Zhar, see that thou now also gettest for me the thrice-lovely Nastasia of the sea."--"But I cannot, sir!" said Tremsin.--"Answer me not so!" replied the nobleman, "for so sure as I've a sword, I'll slice thy head off like a gourd an thou bring her not."--Then Tremsin went out to his horse and fell a-weeping.--"Wherefore dost thou weep?" asked the faithful steed.--"Wherefore should I not weep?" he replied. "My master has given me a task that cannot be done."--"What task is that?"--"Why, to fetch him the thrice-lovely Nastasia of the sea!"--"Oh-ho!" laughed the horse, "that is not a task, but a trifle. Go to thy master and say, 'Cause white tents to be raised by the sea-shore, and buy wares of sundry kinds, and wine and spirits in bottles and flasks,' and the thrice-lovely Nastasia will come and purchase thy wares, and then thou mayst take her."

And the nobleman did so. He caused white tents to be pitched by the sea-shore, and bought kerchiefs and scarves and spread them out gaily, and made great store of wine and brandy in bottles and flasks. Then Tremsin rode toward the tents, and while he was on the way his horse said to him, "Now when I go to graze, do thou lie down and feign to sleep. Then the thrice-lovely Nastasia will appear and say, 'What for thy wares?' but do thou keep silence. But when she begins to taste of the wine and the brandy, then she will go to sleep in the tent, and thou canst catch her easily and hold her fast!" Then Tremsin lay down and feigned to sleep, and forth from the sea came the thrice-lovely Nastasia, and went up to the tents and asked, "Merchant, merchant, what for thy wares?" But he lay there, and moved never a limb. She asked the same thing over and over again, but, getting no answer, went into the tents where stood the flasks and the bottles. She tasted of the wine. How good it was! She tasted of the brandy. That was still better. So from tasting she fell to drinking. First she drank a little, and then she drank a little more, and at last she went asleep in the tent. Then Tremsin seized the thrice-lovely Nastasia and put her behind him on horseback, and carried her off to the nobleman. The nobleman praised Tremsin exceedingly, but the thrice-lovely Nastasia said, "Look now! since thou hast found the feather of the Bird Zhar, and the Bird Zhar herself, since also thou hast found me, thou must now fetch me also my little coral necklace from the sea!" Then Tremsin went out to his faithful steed and wept sorely, and told him all about it. And the horse said to him, "Did I not tell thee that grievous woe would come upon thee if thou didst pick up that feather?" But the horse added, "Come! weep not! after all 'tis not a task, but a trifle." Then they went along by the sea, and the horse said to him, "Let me out to graze, and then keep watch till thou seest a crab come forth from the sea, and then say to him, 'I'll catch thee.'"--So Tremsin let his horse out to graze, and he himself stood by the sea-shore, and watched and watched till he saw a crab come swimming along. Then he said to the crab, "I'll catch thee."--"Oh! seize me not!" said the crab, "but let me get back into the sea, and I'll be of great service to thee."--"Very well," said Tremsin, "but thou must get me from the sea the coral necklace of the thrice-lovely Nastasia," and with that he let the crab go back into the sea again. Then the crab called together all her young crabs, and they collected all the coral and brought it ashore, and gave it to Tremsin. Then the faithful steed came running up, and Tremsin mounted it, and took the coral to the thrice-lovely Nastasia. "Well," said Nastasia, "thou hast got the feather of the Bird Zhar, thou hast got the Bird Zhar itself, thou hast got me my coral, get me now from the sea my herd of wild horses!"--Then Tremsin was sore distressed, and went to his faithful steed and wept bitterly, and told him all about it. "Well," said the horse, "this time 'tis no trifle, but a real hard task. Go now to thy master, and bid him buy twenty hides, and twenty poods[13] of pitch, and twenty poods of flax, and twenty poods of hair."--So Tremsin went to his master and told him, and his master bought it all. Then Tremsin loaded his horse with all this, and to the sea they went together. And when they came to the sea the horse said, "Now lay upon me the hides and the tar and the flax, and lay them in this order--first a hide, and then a pood of tar, and then a pood of flax, and so on, laying them thus till they are all laid." Tremsin did so. "And now," said the horse, "I shall plunge into the sea, and when thou seest a large red wave driving toward the shore, run away till the red wave has passed and thou dost see a white wave coming, and then sit down on the shore and keep watch. I shall then come out of the sea, and after me the whole herd; then thou must strike with the horsehair the horse which gallops immediately after me, and he will not be too strong for thee."--So the faithful steed plunged into the sea, and Tremsin sat down on the shore and watched. The horse swam to a bosquet that rose out of the sea, and there the herd of sea-horses was grazing. When the strong charger of Nastasia saw him and the hides he carried on his back, it set off after him at full tilt, and the whole herd followed the strong charger of Nastasia. They drove the horse with the hides into the sea, and pursued him. Then the strong charger of Nastasia caught up the steed of Tremsin and tore off one of his hides, and began to worry it with his teeth and tear it to fragments as he ran. Then he caught him up a second time, and tore off another hide, and began to worry that in like manner till he had torn it also to shreds; and thus he ran after Tremsin's steed for seventy miles, till he had torn off all the hides, and worried them to bits. But Tremsin sat upon the sea-shore till he saw the large white billow bounding in, and behind the billow came his own horse, and behind his own horse came the thrice-terrible charger of the thrice-lovely Nastasia, with the whole herd at his heels. Tremsin struck him full on the forehead with the twenty poods of hair, and immediately he stood stock still. Then Tremsin threw a halter over him, mounted, and drove the whole

65

herd to the thrice-lovely Nastasia. Nastasia praised Tremsin for his prowess, and said to him, "Well, thou hast got the feather of the Bird Zhar, thou hast got the Bird Zhar itself, thou hast got me my coral and my herd of horses, now milk my mare and put the milk into three vats, so that there may be milk hot as boiling water in the first vat, lukewarm milk in the second vat, and icy cold milk in the third vat." Then Tremsin went to his faithful steed and wept bitterly, and the horse said to him, "Wherefore dost thou weep?"--"Why should I not weep?" cried he; "the thrice-lovely Nastasia has given me a task to do that cannot be done. I am to fill three vats with the milk from her mare, and the milk must be boiling hot in the first vat, and lukewarm in the second, and icy cold in the third vat."--"Oh-ho!" cried the horse, "that is not a task, but a trifle. I'll caress the mare, and then go on nibbling till thou hast milked all three vats full." So Tremsin did so. He milked the three vats full, and the milk in the first vat was boiling hot, and in the second vat warm, and in the third vat freezing cold. When all was ready the thrice-lovely Nastasia said to Tremsin, "Now, leap first of all into the cold vat, and then into the warm vat, and then into the boiling hot vat!"--Tremsin leaped into the first vat, and leaped out again an old man; he leaped into the second vat, and leaped out again a youth; he leaped into the third vat, but when he leaped out again, he was so young and handsome that no pen can describe it, and no tale can tell of it. Then the thrice-lovely Nastasia herself leaped into the vats. She leaped into the first vat, and came out an old woman; she leaped into the second vat, and came out a young maid; but when she leaped out of the third vat, she was so handsome and goodly that no pen can describe it, and no tale can tell of it. Then the thrice-lovely Nastasia made the nobleman leap into the vats. He leaped into the first vat, and became quite old; he leaped into the second vat, and became quite young; he leaped into the third vat, and burst to pieces. Then Tremsin took unto himself the thrice-lovely Nastasia to wife, and they lived happily together on the nobleman's estate, and the evil servants they drove right away.

THE SERPENT-WIFE

THERE was once a gentleman who had a labourer who never went about in company. His fellow-servants did all they could to make him come with them, and now and then enticed him into the tavern, but they could never get him to stay there long, and he always wandered away by himself through the woods. One day he went strolling about in the forest as usual, far from any village and the haunts of men, when he came upon a huge Serpent, which wriggled straight up to him and said, "I am going to eat thee on the spot!" But the labourer, who was used to the loneliness of the forest, replied, "Very well, eat me if thou hast a mind to!"--Then the Serpent said, "Nay! I will not eat thee; only do what I tell thee!" And the Serpent began to tell the man what he had to do. "Turn back home," it said, "and thou wilt find thy master angry because thou hast tarried so long, and there was none to work for him, so that his corn has to remain standing in the field. Then he will send thee to bring in his sheaves, and I'll help thee. Load the wagon well, but don't take quite all the sheaves from the field. Leave one little sheaf behind; more than that thou needst not leave, but that thou must leave. Then beg thy master to let thee have this little sheaf by way of wages. Take no money from him, but that one little sheaf only. Then, when thy master has given thee this sheaf, burn it, and a fair lady will leap out of it; take her to wife!"

The labourer obeyed, and went and worked for his master as the Serpent had told him. He went out into the field to bring home his master's corn, and marvellously he managed it. He did all the carrying himself, and loaded the wagon so heavily that it creaked beneath its burden. Then when he had brought home all his master's corn, he begged that he might have the remaining little sheaf for himself. He refused to be rewarded for his smart labour, he would take no money; he wanted nothing for himself, he said, but the little sheaf he had left in the field. So his master let him have the sheaf. Then he went out by himself into the field, burnt the sheaf, just as the Serpent had told him, and immediately a lovely lady leapt out of it. The labourer forthwith took and married her; and now he began to look out for a place to build him a hut upon. His master gave him a place where he might build his hut, and his wife helped him so much with the building of it that it seemed to him as if he himself never laid a hand to it. His hut grew up as quick as thought, and it contained everything that they wanted. The man could not understand it; he could only walk about and wonder at it. Wherever he looked there was everything quite spick and span and ready for use: none in the whole village had a better house than he.

And so he might have lived in all peace and prosperity to the end of his days had not his desires outstripped his deserts. He had three fields of standing corn, and when he came home one day his labourers said to him, "Thy corn is not gathered in yet, though it is standing all ripe on its stalks." Now the season was getting on, and for all the care and labour of his wife, the corn was still standing in the field. "Why, what's the meaning of this?" thought he. Then in his anger he cried, "I see how it is. Once a serpent, always a serpent!" He was quite beside himself all the way home, and was very wrath with his wife because of the corn.

When he got home he went straight to his chamber to lie down on his pillow. There was no sign of his wife, but a huge serpent was just coiling itself round and round and settling down in the middle of the pillow. Then he called to mind how, once, his wife had said to him, "Beware, for Heaven's sake, of ever calling me a serpent. I will not suffer thee to call me by that name, and if thou dost thou shalt lose thy wife." He called this to mind now, but it was already too late; what he had said could not be unsaid. Then he reflected what a good wife he had had, and how she herself had sought him out, and how she had waited upon him continually and done him boundless good, and yet he had not been able to refrain his tongue, so that now, maybe, he would be without a wife for the rest of his days. His heart grew heavy within him as he thought of all this, and he wept bitterly at the harm he had done to himself. Then the Serpent said to him, "Weep no more. What is to be, must be. Is it thy standing corn thou art grieved about? Go up to thy barn, and there thou wilt find all thy corn lying, to the very last little grain. Have I not brought it all home and threshed it for thee, and set everything in order? And now I must depart to the place where thou didst first find me." Then she crept off, and the man followed her, weeping and mourning all the time as for one already dead. When they reached the forest she stopped and coiled herself round and round beneath a hazel-nut bush. Then she said to the man, "Now kiss me once, but see to it that I do not bite thee!"--Then he kissed her once, and she wound herself round a branch of a tree and asked him, "What dost thou feel within thee?"--He answered, "At the moment when I kissed thee it seemed to me as if I knew everything that was going on in the world!"--Then she said to him again, "Kiss me a second time!"--"And what dost thou feel now?" she asked when he had kissed her again.--"Now," said he, "I understand all languages which are spoken among men."-- Then she said to him, "And now kiss me a third time, but this will be for the last time." Then he kissed the Serpent for the last time, and she said to him, "What dost thou feel now?"--"Now," said he, "I know all that is going on under the earth."--"Go now," said she, "to the Tsar, and he will give thee his daughter for the knowledge thou hast. But pray to God for poor me, for now I must be and remain a serpent for ever." And with that the Serpent uncoiled herself and disappeared among the bushes, but the man went away and wedded the Tsar's daughter.

R. Nisbet Bain

THE STORY OF UNLUCKY DANIEL

THERE was once upon a time a youth called Unlucky Dan. Wherever he went, and whatever he did, and with whomsoever he served, nothing came of it: all his labour was like spilt water, he got no good from it. One day he took service with a new master. "I'll serve thee a whole year," said he, "for a piece of sown wheat-land." His master agreed, and he entered into his service, and at the same time he sowed his piece of wheat-land. His wheat shot up rapidly. When his master's wheat was in the stalk, his was already in the ear, and when his master's wheat was in the ear, his own wheat was already ripe. "I'll reap it to-morrow," thought he. The same night a cloud arose, the hail poured down, and destroyed his wheat altogether. Daniel fell a-weeping. "I'll go serve another master," he cried, "perhaps God will then prosper me!" So he went to another master. "I'll serve thee for a whole year," said he, "if thou wilt give me that wild colt." So he stopped and served him, and by the end of the year he trained the wild colt so well that he made a carriage-horse out of it. "Oh-ho!" thought he, "I shall take away something with me this time!" The same night the wolves made an inroad upon the stables and tore the horse to pieces. Daniel fell a-weeping. "I'll go to another master," said he, "perhaps I shall be luckier there." So he went to a third master, and on this master's tomb lay a large stone. Whence it came none knew, and it was so heavy that none could move it, though they tried for ages. "I'll serve thee a year," said he, "for that stone." The master agreed, and he entered his service. Then a change came over the stone, and divers flowers began to grow upon it. On one side they were red, on the second side silver, and on the third side golden. "Oh-ho," thought Daniel, "that stone, at any rate, will soon be mine. Nobody can move it."

71

But the next morning a thunderbolt descended and struck the stone, and shivered it to atoms. Then Daniel fell a-weeping, and lamented that God had given him nothing, though he had served for so many years. But the people said to him, "Listen now! thou that art so unlucky, why dost thou not go to the Tsar? He is the father of us all, and will therefore certainly care for thee!" So he listened to them and went, and the Tsar gave him a place at his court. One day the Tsar said to him, "I marvel that thou art so unlucky, for do whatsoever thou wilt, thou art none the better for it. I would fain requite thee for all thy labours." Then he took and filled three barrels, the first with gold, and the second with coal, and the third with sand, and said to Daniel, "Look now! if thou dost pitch upon that which is filled with gold, thou shalt be a Tsar; if thou dost choose the one that is filled with coal, thou shalt be a blacksmith; but if thou dost pick out the one that is full of sand, why then thou art indeed hopelessly unlucky, and out of my tsardom thou must go straightway, yet I will give thee a horse and armour to take along with thee." So Daniel was brought to the place where were the three barrels, and went about them and felt and felt them one after the other. "This one is full of gold!" said he. They broke it open and it was full of sand. "Well," said the Tsar, "I see that thou art hopelessly unlucky. Depart from my tsardom, for I have no need at all of such as thou." Then he gave him a charger and armour, and the full equipment of a Cossack, and sent him away.

He went on and on for a whole day, he went on and on for a second day, and there was nothing to eat, either for his horse or himself. He went for a third day, and in the distance he saw a hay-cock. "That will do for my horse, at any rate," thought he, "even if it is of no good to me." So he went up to it, and immediately it burst into flames. Daniel began to weep, when he heard a voice crying piteously, "Save me, save me! I am burning!"--"How can I save thee," he cried, "when I myself cannot draw near?"--"Oh! give me thy weapon!" cried the voice, "and I'll seize hold of it, and then thou canst pull me out." So he stretched forth his weapon, and drew forth a goodly serpent, such as is only known of in old folk-songs. And she said to him, "Since thou hast drawn me out, thou must also take me home."--"How shall I carry thee?" asked he.--"Carry me on thy horse, and in whatsoever direction I turn my head and his, thither go."--So he took her upon his horse, and they went on and on till they came to a court so splendid that it was a delight to look at it. Then she glided down from his charger and said, "Wait here, and I'll soon be with thee again," and with that she wriggled under the gate. He stood there and stood and waited and waited till he wept from sheer weariness; but, at last, she came out again in the shape of a lovely damsel in gorgeous raiment, and opened the gate for him. "Lead in thy horse," said she, "and eat and rest awhile." So they went into the courtyard, and in the midst of it stood two springs. The lady drew out of one of these springs a little glass of water, and strewing a handful of oats beside it, said, "Fasten up thy horse here!"--"What!" thought he, "for these three days we have had naught to eat or drink, and now she mocks us with a handful of oats!"--Then they went together to the guest-chamber, and she gave him there a little glass of water and a small piece of wheaten bread.--"Why, what is this for a hungry man like me?" thought he. But when he chanced to glance through the window, he saw that the whole courtyard was full of oats and water, and that his horse had already eaten its fill. Then he nibbled his little piece of wheaten bread and sipped his water, and his hunger was immediately satisfied. "Well," said the lady, "hast thou eaten thy fill?"--"That I have," he replied.--"Then lie down and rest awhile," said she. And the next morning, when he rose up, she said to him, "Give me thy horse, thy armour, and thy raiment, and I'll give thee mine in exchange."--Then she gave him her shift and her weapon, and said, "This sword is of such a sort that, if thou do but wave it, all men will fall down before thee; and as for this shift, when once thou hast it on, none will be able to seize thee. And now go on thy way till thou come to an inn, and there they will tell thee that the Tsar of that land is seeking warriors. Go and offer thyself to him, and thou shalt marry his daughter, but

DANIEL WAVED HIS SWORD

tell her not the truth for seven years!" Then they took leave of each other, and he departed. He came to the inn, and there they asked him whence he came. And when they knew that he came from a strange land, they said to him, "A strange people has attacked our Tsar, and he cannot defend himself, for a mighty warrior has conquered his tsardom and carried off his daughter, and worries him to death."--"Show me the way to your Tsar," said Daniel. Then they showed him, and he went. When he came to the Tsar, he said to him, "I will subdue this strange land for thee. All the army I want is a couple of Cossacks, but they must be picked men." Then the heralds went through the tsardom till they had found these two Cossacks, and Daniel went forth with them into the endless steppes, and there he bade them lie down and sleep while he kept watch. And while they slept the army of the strange country came upon them, and cried to Daniel to turn back if he would escape destruction. And then they began to fire with their guns and cannons, and they fired so many balls that the bodies of the two Cossacks were quite covered by them. Then Daniel waved his sword and smote, and only those whom his blows did not reach escaped alive. So he vanquished them all, and conquered that strange land, and came back and married the Tsar's daughter, and they lived happily together.

But counsellors from the strange land whispered dark sayings in the ears of the Tsarivna. "What is this fellow that thou hast taken to thyself? Who is he, and whence? Find out for us wherein lies his strength, that we may destroy him and take thee away."-- Then she began asking him, and he said to her, "Look now! all my strength is in these gloves." Then she waited till he was asleep, and drew them off him, and gave them to the people from the strange land. And the next day he went hunting, and the evil counsellors surrounded and shot at him with their darts, and beat him with the gloves; but it was all in vain. Then he waved his sword, and whomsoever he struck fell to the ground, and he clapped them all in prison.

But his wife caressed and wheedled him again, and said, "Nay, but tell me, wherein doth thy strength lie?"--"My strength, darling," said he, "lies in my boots." Then she drew off his boots while he slept, and gave them to his enemies. And they fell upon him again as he went out, but again he waved his sword, and as many as he struck fell to the ground, and he put them all in prison. Then his wife wheedled and caressed him the third time. "Nay, but tell me, darling," quoth she, "wherein doth thy strength lie?" Then he was wearied with her beseeching, and said to her, "My strength lies in this sword of mine, and in my shirt, and so long as I have this shirt on, nobody can touch me." Then she caressed and fondled him, and said, "Thou shouldst take a bath, my darling, and well wash thyself. My father always did so." So he let himself be persuaded, and no sooner had he undressed than she changed all his clothes for others, and gave his sword and his shirt to his enemies. Then he came out of his bath, and immediately they fell upon him, cut him to pieces, put him in a sack, placed him on his horse, and let the horse go where it would. So the horse went on and on, and wandered farther and farther, till it came to the old place where he had stayed with the Serpent Lady. And when his benefactress saw him, she said, "Why, if poor unlucky Daniel hasn't fallen into a scrape again." And immediately she took him out of the sack, and fitted his pieces together, and washed them clean, and took healing water from one of the springs, and living water from the other, and sprinkled him all over, and he stood there sound and strong again. "Now, did I not bid thee tell not thy wife the truth for seven years?" said she, "and thou wouldst not take heed." And he stood there, and spoke never a word. "Well, now, rest awhile," she continued, "for thou dost need it, and then I'll give thee something else." So the next day she gave him a chain, and said to him, "Listen! Go to that inn where thou didst go before, and early next morning, whilst thou art bathing, bid the innkeeper beat thee with all his might on the back with this chain, and so thou wilt get back to thy wife, but tell her not a word of what has happened." So he went to this same inn and passed the night there, and, on the morrow, he called the innkeeper, and said to him, "Look now! the first time I dip my head in the water, beat me about the back with this chain as hard as thou canst." So the innkeeper waited till he had ducked his head under the water, and then he thrashed him with the chain, whereupon he turned into a horse so beautiful that it was a delight to look upon it. The innkeeper was so glad, so glad. "So I've got rid of one guest only to get another one," thought he. He lost no time in taking the horse to the fair, and offered it for sale, and among those who saw it was the Tsar himself. "What dost thou ask for it?" said the Tsar.--"I ask five thousand roubles." Then the Tsar counted down the money and took the horse away. When he got to his court, he made a great to-do about his beautiful horse, and cried to his daughter, "Come and see, dear little heart, what a fine horse I have bought." Then she came forth to look at it; but the moment she saw it, she cried, "That horse will be my ruin. Thou must kill it on the spot."--"Nay, dear little heart! how can I do such a thing?" said the Tsar.--"Slay it thou must, and slay it thou shalt!" cried the Tsarivna. So they sent for a knife, and began sharpening it, when one of the maidens of the court took pity on the horse, and cried, "Oh, my good, my darling horse, so lovely as thou art, and yet to kill thee!" But the horse neighed and went to her, and said, "Look now! take the first drop of blood which flows from me, and bury it in the garden." Then they slew the horse, but the maiden did as she was told, and took the drop of blood and buried it in the garden. And from this drop of blood there sprang up a cherry-tree; and its first leaf was golden, and its second leaf was of richer colour still, and its third leaf was yet another colour, and every leaf upon it was different to the others. One day the Tsar went out walking in his garden, and when he saw this cherry-tree he fell in love with it, and praised it to his daughter. "Look!" said he, "what a beauteous cherry-tree we have in our garden! Who can tell whence it sprung?"--But the moment the Tsarivna saw it, she cried, "That tree will be my ruin! Thou must cut it down."--"Nay!" said he, "how can I cut down the fairest ornament of my garden?"--"Down it must come, and down it shall come!" replied the

HIS WIFE CARESSED AND WHEEDLED HIM

Tsarivna. Then they sent for an axe and made ready to cut it down, but the damsel came running up, and said, "Oh, darling little cherry-tree, darling little cherry-tree, so fair thou art! From a horse hast thou sprung, and now they will fell thee before thou hast lived a day!"--"Never mind," said the cherry-tree; "take the first chip that falls from me, and throw it into the water."--Then they cut down the cherry-tree; but the girl did as she was bidden, and threw the first chip from the cherry-tree into the water, and out of it swam a drake so beautiful that it was a delight to look upon it. Then the Tsar went a-hunting, and saw it swimming in the water, and it was so close that he could touch it with his hand. The Tsar took off his clothes and plunged into the water after it, and it enticed him farther and farther away from the shore. Then the drake swam toward the spot where the Tsar had left his clothes, and when it came up to them it changed into a man and put them on, and behold! the man was Daniel. Then he called to the Tsar: "Swim hither, swim hither!" The Tsar swam up, but when he swam ashore Daniel met and killed him, and after that he went back to court in the Tsar's clothes. Then all the courtiers hailed him as the Tsar, but he said, "Where is that damsel who was here just now?"--They brought her instantly before him. "Well," said he to her, "thou hast been a second mother to me, and now thou shalt be my second wife!" So he lived with her and was happy, but he caused his first wife to be tied to the tails of wild horses and torn to pieces in the endless steppes.

R. NISBET BAIN

THE SPARROW AND THE BUSH

A SPARROW once flew down upon a bush and said, "Little bush, give good little sparrow a swing."--"I won't!" said the little bush. Then the sparrow was angry, and went to the goat and said, "Goat, goat, nibble bush, bush won't give good little sparrow a swing."--"I won't!" said the goat.--Then the sparrow went to the wolf and said, "Wolf, wolf, eat goat, goat won't nibble bush, bush won't give good little sparrow a swing."--"I won't!" said the wolf.--Then the sparrow went to the people and said, "Good people, kill wolf, wolf won't eat goat, goat won't nibble bush, bush won't give good little sparrow a swing."--"We won't!" said the people.--Then the sparrow went to the Tartars and said, "Tartars, Tartars, slay people, people won't kill wolf, wolf won't eat goat, goat won't nibble bush, bush won't give good little sparrow a swing."--But the Tartars said, "We won't slay the people!" and the people said, "We won't kill the wolf!" and the wolf said, "I won't eat the goat!" and the goat said, "I won't nibble the bush!" and the bush said, "I won't give the good little sparrow a swing."--"Go!" said the bush, "to the fire, for the Tartars won't slay the people, and the people won't kill the wolf, and the wolf won't eat the goat, and the goat won't nibble the bush, and the bush won't give the dear little sparrow a swing."--But the fire also said, "I won't!" (they were all alike)--"go to the water," said he.--So the sparrow went to the water and said, "Come water, quench fire, fire won't burn Tartars, Tartars won't slay people, people won't kill wolf, wolf won't eat goat, goat won't nibble bush, bush won't give good little sparrow a swing."--But the water also said, "I won't!" So the sparrow went to the ox and said, "Ox, ox, drink water, water won't quench fire, fire won't burn Tartars, Tartars won't slay people, people won't kill wolf, wolf

81

won't eat goat, goat won't nibble bush, bush won't give little sparrow a swing."--"I won't!" said the ox.--Then the sparrow went to the pole-axe and said, "Pole-axe, pole-axe, strike ox, ox won't drink water, water won't quench fire, fire won't burn Tartars, Tartars won't slay people, people won't kill wolf, wolf won't eat goat, goat won't nibble bush, bush won't give little sparrow a swing."--"I won't!" said the pole-axe.--So the sparrow went to the worms and said, "Worms, worms, gnaw pole-axe, pole-axe won't strike ox, ox won't drink water, water won't quench fire, fire won't burn Tartars, Tartars won't slay people, people won't kill wolf, wolf won't eat goat, goat won't nibble bush, bush won't give little sparrow a swing."--"We won't!" said the worms.--Then the sparrow went to the hen and said, "Hen, hen, peck worms, worms won't gnaw pole-axe, pole-axe won't strike ox, ox won't drink water, water won't quench fire, fire won't burn Tartars, Tartars won't slay people, people won't kill wolf, wolf won't eat goat, goat won't nibble bush, bush won't give little sparrow a swing."--"I won't!" said the hen, "but go to the sparrow-hawk, he ought to give the first push, or why is he called the Pusher!"[14]--So the sparrow went to the sparrow-hawk and said, "Come, pusher, seize hen, hen won't peck worms, worms won't gnaw pole-axe, pole-axe won't strike ox, ox won't drink water, water won't quench fire, fire won't burn Tartars, Tartars won't slay people, people won't kill wolf, wolf won't eat goat, goat won't nibble bush, bush won't give little sparrow a swing."

Then the sparrow-hawk began to seize the hen, the hen began to peck the worms, the worms began to gnaw the pole-axe, the pole-axe began to hit the ox, the ox began to drink the water, the water began to quench the fire, the fire began to burn the Tartars, the Tartars began to slay the people, the people began to kill the wolf, the wolf began to eat the goat, the goat began to nibble the bush, and the bush cried out:

> "*Swing away, swing away, swi-i-i-ing!*
> *Little daddy sparrow, have your fli-i-i-ing!*"

THE OLD DOG

THERE was once a man who had a dog. While the dog was young he was made much of, but when he grew old he was driven out of doors. So he went and lay outside the fence, and a wolf came up to him and said, "Doggy, why so down in the mouth?"--"While I was young," said the dog, "they made much of me; but now that I am old they beat me." The wolf said, "I see thy master in the field; go after him, and perchance he'll give thee something."--"Nay," said the dog, "they won't even let me walk about the fields now, they only beat me."--"Look now," said the wolf, "I'm sorry, and will make things better for thee. Thy mistress, I see, has put her child down beneath that wagon. I'll seize it, and make off with it. Run thou after me and bark, and though thou hast no teeth left, touzle me as much as thou canst, so that thy mistress may see it."

So the wolf seized the child, and ran away with it, and the dog ran after him, and began to touzle him. His mistress saw it, and made after them with a harrow, crying at the same time, "Husband, husband! the wolf has got the child! Gabriel, Gabriel! don't you see? The wolf has got the child!" Then the man chased the wolf, and got back the child. "Brave old dog!" said he; "you are old and toothless, and yet you can give help in time of need, and will not let your master's child be stolen." And henceforth the woman and her husband gave the old dog a large lump of bread every day.

R. Nisbet Bain

THE FOX AND THE CAT

IN a certain forest there once lived a fox, and near to the fox lived a man who had a cat that had been a good mouser in its youth, but was now old and half blind. The man didn't want puss any longer, but not liking to kill it, took it out into the forest and lost it there. Then the fox came up and said, "Why, Mr Shaggy Matthew! How d'ye do! What brings you here?"--"Alas!" said Pussy, "my master loved me as long as I could bite, but now that I can bite no longer and have left off catching mice--and I used to catch them finely once--he doesn't like to kill me, but he has left me in the wood where I must perish miserably."--"No, dear Pussy!" said the fox; "you leave it to me, and I'll help you to get your daily bread."--"You are very good, dear little sister foxey!" said the cat, and the fox built him a little shed with a garden round it to walk about in.

Now one day the hare came to steal the man's cabbage. "Kreem-kreem-kreem!" he squeaked. But the cat popped his head out of the window, and when he saw the hare, he put up his back and stuck up his tail and said, "Ft-t-t-t-Frrrrrrr!" The hare was frightened and ran away and told the bear, the wolf, and the wild boar all about it. "Never mind," said the bear, "I tell you what, we'll all four give a banquet, and invite the fox and the cat, and do for the pair of them. Now, look here! I'll steal the man's mead; and you, Mr Wolf, steal his fat-pot; and you, Mr Wildboar, root up his fruit-trees; and you, Mr Bunny, go and invite the fox and the cat to dinner."

So they made everything ready as the bear had said, and the hare ran off to invite the guests. He came beneath the window and said, "We invite your little ladyship Foxey-Woxey, together with

Mr Shaggy Matthew, to dinner"--and back he ran again.--"But you should have told them to bring their spoons with them," said the bear.--"Oh, what a head I've got! if I didn't quite forget!" cried the hare, and back he went again, ran beneath the window and cried, "Mind you bring your spoons!"--"Very well," said the fox.

So the cat and the fox went to the banquet, and when the cat saw the bacon, he put up his back and stuck out his tail, and cried, "Mee-oo, mee-oo!" with all his might. But they thought he said, "Ma-lo, ma-lo[15]!"--"What!" said the bear, who was hiding behind the beeches with the other beasts, "here have we four been getting together all we could, and this pig-faced cat calls it too little! What a monstrous cat he must be to have such an appetite!" So they were all four very frightened, and the bear ran up a tree, and the others hid where they could. But when the cat saw the boar's bristles sticking out from behind the bushes he thought it was a mouse, and put up his back again and cried, "Ft! ft! ft! Frrrrrrr!" Then they were more frightened than ever. And the boar went into a bush still farther off, and the wolf went behind an oak, and the bear got down from the tree, and climbed up into a bigger one, and the hare ran right away.

But the cat remained in the midst of all the good things and ate away at the bacon, and the little fox gobbled up the honey, and they ate and ate till they couldn't eat any more, and then they both went home licking their paws.

THE STRAW OX

THERE was once upon a time an old man and an old woman. The old man worked in the fields as a pitch-burner, while the old woman sat at home and spun flax. They were so poor that they could save nothing at all; all their earnings went in bare food, and when that was gone there was nothing left. At last the old woman had a good idea. "Look now, husband," cried she, "make me a straw ox, and smear it all over with tar."--"Why, you foolish woman!" said he, "what's the good of an ox of that sort?"--"Never mind," said she, "you just make it. I know what I am about."--What was the poor man to do? He set to work and made the ox of straw, and smeared it all over with tar.

The night passed away, and at early dawn the old woman took her distaff, and drove the straw ox out into the steppe to graze, and she herself sat down behind a hillock, and began spinning her flax, and cried, "Graze away, little ox, while I spin my flax! Graze away, little ox, while I spin my flax!" And while she spun, her head drooped down and she began to doze, and while she was dozing, from behind the dark wood and from the back of the huge pines a bear came rushing out upon the ox and said, "Who are you? Speak and tell me!"--And the ox said, "A three-year-old heifer am I, made of straw and smeared with tar."--"Oh!" said the bear, "stuffed with straw and trimmed with tar, are you? Then give me of your straw and tar, that I may patch up my ragged fur again!"--"Take some," said the ox, and the bear fell upon him and began to tear away at the tar. He tore and tore, and buried his teeth in it till he found he couldn't let go again. He tugged and he tugged, but it was no good, and the ox dragged him gradually off goodness knows where. Then the old woman awoke, and there

87

was no ox to be seen. "Alas! old fool that I am!" cried she, "perchance it has gone home." Then she quickly caught up her distaff and spinning-board, threw them over her shoulders, and hastened off home, and she saw that the ox had dragged the bear up to the fence, and in she went to the old man. "Dad, dad!" she cried, "look, look! the ox has brought us a bear. Come out and kill it!" Then the old man jumped up, tore off the bear, tied him up, and threw him in the cellar.

Next morning, between dark and dawn, the old woman took her distaff and drove the ox into the steppe to graze. She herself sat down by a mound, began spinning, and said, "Graze, graze away, little ox, while I spin my flax! Graze, graze away, little ox, while I spin my flax!" And while she spun, her head drooped down and she dozed. And, lo! from behind the dark wood, from the back of the huge pines, a grey wolf came rushing out upon the ox and said, "Who are you? Come, tell me!"--"I am a three-year-old heifer, stuffed with straw and trimmed with tar," said the ox.--"Oh! trimmed with tar, are you? Then give me of your tar to tar my sides, that the dogs and the sons of dogs tear me not!"--"Take some," said the ox. And with that the wolf fell upon him and tried to tear the tar off. He tugged and tugged, and tore with his teeth, but could get none off. Then he tried to let go, and couldn't; tug and worry as he might, it was no good. When the old woman woke, there was no heifer in sight. "Maybe my heifer has gone home!" she cried; "I'll go home and see." When she got there she was astonished, for by the palings stood the ox with the wolf still tugging at it. She ran and told her old man, and her old man came and threw the wolf into the cellar also.

On the third day the old woman again drove her ox into the pastures to graze, and sat down by a mound and dozed off. Then a fox came running up. "Who are you?" it asked the ox.--"I'm a three-year-old heifer, stuffed with straw and daubed with tar."--"Then give me some of your tar to smear my sides with, when those dogs and sons of dogs tear my hide!"--"Take some," said the ox. Then the fox fastened her teeth in him and couldn't draw them out again. The old woman told her old man, and he took and cast the fox into the cellar in the same way. And after that they caught Pussy Swift-foot[16] likewise.

So when he had got them all safely, the old man sat down on a bench before the cellar and began sharpening a knife. And the bear said to him, "Tell me, daddy, what are you sharpening your knife for?"--"To flay your skin off, that I may make a leather jacket for myself and a pelisse for my old wife."--"Oh! don't flay me, daddy dear! Rather let me go, and I'll bring you a lot of honey."--"Very well, see you do it," and he unbound and let the bear go. Then he sat down on the bench and again began sharpening his knife. And the wolf asked him, "Daddy, what are you sharpening your knife for?"--"To flay off your skin, that I may make me a warm cap against the winter."--"Oh! don't flay me, daddy dear, and I'll bring you a whole herd of little sheep."-- "Well, see that you do it," and he let the wolf go. Then he sat down and began sharpening his knife again. The fox put out her little snout and asked him, "Be so kind, dear daddy, and tell me why you are sharpening your knife!"--"Little foxes," said the old man, "have nice skins that do capitally for collars and trimmings, and I want to skin you!"--"Oh! don't take my skin away, daddy dear, and I will bring you hens and geese."--"Very well, see that you do it!" and he let the fox go. The hare now alone remained, and the old man began sharpening his knife on the hare's account. "Why do you do that?" asked puss, and he replied, "Little hares have nice little soft warm skins, which will make me gloves and mittens against the winter!"--"Oh! daddy dear! don't flay me, and I'll bring you kale and good cauliflower, if only you let me go!" Then he let the hare go also.

Then they went to bed, but very early in the morning, when it was neither dusk nor dawn, there was a noise in the doorway like "Durrrrrr!"--"Daddy!" cried the old woman, "there's some one scratching at the door, go and see who it is!" The old man went out, and there was the bear carrying a whole hive full of honey. The old man took the honey from the bear, but no sooner did he lie down than again there was another "Durrrrr!" at the door. The old man looked out and saw the wolf driving a whole flock of sheep into the yard. Close on his heels came the fox, driving before him geese and hens and all manner of fowls; and last of all came the hare, bringing cabbage and kale and all manner of good food. And the old man was glad, and the old woman was glad. And the old man sold the sheep and oxen and got so rich that he needed nothing more. As for the straw-stuffed ox, it stood in the sun till it fell to pieces.

THE GOLDEN SLIPPER

THERE was once upon a time an old man and an old woman, and the old man had a daughter, and the old woman had a daughter. And the old woman said to the old man, "Go and buy a heifer, that thy daughter may have something to look after!" So the old man went to the fair and bought a heifer.

Now the old woman spoiled her own daughter, but was always snapping at the old man's daughter. Yet the old man's daughter was a good, hard-working girl, while as for the old woman's daughter, she was but an idle slut. She did nothing but sit down all day with her hands in her lap. One day the old woman said to the old man's daughter, "Look now, thou daughter of a dog, go and drive out the heifer to graze! Here thou hast two bundles of flax. See that thou unravel it, and reel it, and bleach it, and bring it home all ready in the evening!" Then the girl took the flax and drove the heifer out to graze.

So the heifer began to graze, but the girl sat down and began to weep. And the heifer said to her, "Tell me, dear little maiden, wherefore dost thou weep?"--"Alas! why should I not weep? My stepmother has given me this flax and bidden me unravel it, and reel it, and bleach it, and bring it back as cloth in the evening."-- "Grieve not, maiden!" said the heifer, "it will all turn out well. Lie down to sleep!"--So she lay down to sleep, and when she awoke the flax was all unravelled and reeled and spun into fine cloth, and bleached. Then she drove the heifer home and gave the cloth to her stepmother. The old woman took it and hid it away, that nobody might know that the old man's daughter had brought it to her.

THE GIRL DROVE THE HEIFER OUT TO GRAZE

The next day she said to her own daughter, "Dear little daughter, drive the heifer out to graze, and here is a little piece of flax for thee, unravel it and reel it, or unravel it not and reel it not as thou likest best, but bring it home with thee." Then she drove the heifer out to graze, and threw herself down in the grass, and slept the whole day, and did not even take the trouble to go and moisten the flax in the cooling stream. And in the evening she drove the heifer back from the field and gave her mother the flax. "Oh, mammy!" she said, "my head ached so the whole day, and the sun scorched so, that I couldn't go down to the stream to moisten the flax."--"Never mind," said her mother, "lie down and sleep; it will do for another day."

And the next day she called the old man's daughter again, "Get up, thou daughter of a dog, and take the heifer out to graze. And here thou hast a bundle of raw flax; unravel it, heckle it, wind it on to thy spindles, bleach it, weave with it, and make it into fine cloth for me by the evening!"--Then the girl drove out the heifer to graze. The heifer began grazing, but she sat down beneath a willow-tree, and threw her flax down beside her, and began weeping with all her might. But the heifer came up to her and said, "Tell me, little maiden, wherefore dost thou weep?"--"Why should I not weep?" said she, and she told the heifer all about it.-- "Grieve not!" said the heifer, "it will all come right, but lie down to sleep."--So she lay down and immediately fell asleep. And by evening the bundle of raw flax was heckled and spun and reeled, and the cloth was woven and bleached, so that one could have made shirts of it straight off. Then she drove the heifer home, and gave the cloth to her stepmother.

Then the old woman said to herself, "How comes it that this daughter of the son of a dog has done all her task so easily? The heifer must have got it done for her, I know. But I'll put a stop to all this, thou daughter of the son of a dog," said she. Then she went to the old man and said, "Father, kill and cut to pieces this heifer of thine, for because of it thy daughter does not a stroke of work.

She drives the heifer out to graze, and goes to sleep the whole day and does nothing."--"Then I'll kill it!" said he.--But the old man's daughter heard what he said, and went into the garden and began to weep bitterly. The heifer came to her and said, "Tell me, dear little maiden, wherefore dost thou weep?"--"Why should I *not* weep," she said, "when they want to kill thee?"--"Don't grieve," said the heifer, "it will all come right. When they have killed me, ask thy stepmother to give thee my entrails to wash, and in them thou wilt find a grain of corn. Plant this grain of corn, and out of it will grow up a willow-tree, and whatever thou dost want, go to this willow-tree and ask, and thou shalt have thy heart's desire."

Then her father slew the heifer, and she went to her stepmother and said, "Prythee, let me have the entrails of the heifer to wash!"--And her stepmother answered, "As if I would let anybody else do such work but thee!"--Then she went and washed them, and sure enough she found the grain of corn, planted it by the porch, trod down the earth, and watered it a little. And the next morning, when she awoke, she saw that a willow-tree had sprung out of this grain of corn, and beneath the willow-tree was a spring of water, and no better water was to be found anywhere in the whole village. It was as cold and as clear as ice.

When Sunday came round, the old woman tricked her pet daughter out finely, and took her to church, but to the old man's daughter she said, "Look to the fire, thou slut! Keep a good fire burning and get ready the dinner, and make everything in the house neat and tidy, and have thy best frock on, and all the shirts washed against I come back from church. And if thou hast not all these things done, thou shalt say good-bye to dear life."

So the old woman and her daughter went to church, and the smart little stepdaughter made the fire burn up, and got the dinner ready, and then went to the willow-tree and said, "Willow-tree, willow-tree, come out of thy bark! Lady Anna, come when I call thee!" Then the willow-tree did its duty, and shook all its leaves, and a noble lady came forth from it. "Dear little lady, sweet little lady, what are thy commands?" said she.--"Give me," said she, "a grand dress and let me have a carriage and horses, for I would go to God's House!"--And immediately she was dressed in silk and satin, with golden slippers on her feet, and the carriage came up and she went to church.

When she entered the church there was a great to-do, and every one said, "Oh! oh! oh! Who is it? Is it perchance some princess or some queen? for the like of it we have never seen before." Now the young Tsarevich chanced to be in church at that time. When he saw her, his heart began to beat. He stood there, and could not take his eyes off her. And all the great captains and courtiers marvelled at her and fell in love with her straightway. But who she was, they knew not. When service was over, she got up and drove away. When she got home, she took off all her fine things, and put on all her rags again, and sat in the window-corner and watched the folk coming from church.

Then her stepmother came back too. "Is the dinner ready?" said she.--"Yes, it is ready."--"Hast thou sewn the shirts?"--"Yes, the shirts are sewn too."--Then they sat down to meat, and began to relate how they had seen such a beautiful young lady at church.-- "The Tsarevich," said the old woman, "instead of saying his prayers, was looking at her all the while, so goodly was she." Then she said to the old man's daughter, "As for thee, thou slut! though thou *hast* sewn the shirts and bleached them, thou art but a dirty under-wench!"

On the following Sunday the stepmother again dressed up her daughter, and took her to church. But, before she went, she said to the old man's daughter, "See that thou keep the fire in, thou slut!" and she gave her a lot of work to do. The old man's daughter very soon did it all, and then she went to the willow-tree and said,

"Bright spring willow, bright spring willow, change thee, transform thee!" Then still statelier dames stepped forth from the willow-tree, "Dear little lady, sweet little lady, what commands hast thou to give?" She told them what she wanted, and they gave her a gorgeous dress, and put golden shoes on her feet, and she went to church in a grand carriage. The Tsarevich was again there, and at the sight of her he stood as if rooted to the ground, and couldn't take his eyes from her. Then the people began to whisper, "Is there none here who knows her? Is there none who knows who such a handsome lady may be!" And they began to ask each other, "Dost *thou* know her? Dost *thou* know her?"--But the Tsarevich said, "Whoever will tell me who this great lady is, to him will I give a sack-load of gold ducats!"--Then they inquired and inquired, and laid all their heads together, but nothing came of it. But the Tsarevich had a jester who was always with him, and used always to jest and cut capers whenever this child of the Tsar was sad. So now, too, he began to laugh at the young Tsarevich and say to him, "I know how to find out who this fine lady is."--"How?" asked the young Tsarevich.--"I'll tell thee," said the jester; "smear with pitch the place in church where she is wont to stand. Then her slippers will stick to it, and she, in her hurry to get away, will never notice that she has left them behind her in church."--So the Tsarevich ordered his courtiers to smear the spot with pitch straightway. Next time, when the service was over, she got up as usual and hastened away, but left her golden slippers behind her. When she got home she took off her costly raiment and put on her rags, and waited in the window-corner till they came from church.

When they came from church they had all sorts of things to talk about, and how the young Tsarevich had fallen in love with the grand young lady, and how they were unable to tell him whence she came, or who she was, and the stepmother hated the old man's daughter all the more because she had done her work so nicely.

But the Tsarevich did nothing but pine away. And they proclaimed throughout the kingdom, "Who has lost a pair of golden slippers?" But none could tell. Then the Tsar sent his wise councillors throughout the kingdom to find her. "If ye do not find her," said he, "it will be the death of my child, and then ye also are dead men."

So the Tsar's councillors went through all the towns and villages, and measured the feet of all the maidens against the golden slippers, and she was to be the bride of the Tsarevich whom the golden slippers fitted. They went to the houses of all the princes, and all the nobles, and all the rich merchants, but it was of no avail. The feet of all the maidens were either too little or too large. Then they hied them to the huts of the peasants.

They went on and on, they measured and measured, and at last they were so tired that they could scarce draw one foot after the other. Then they looked about them and saw a beautiful willow-tree standing by a hut, and beneath the willow-tree was a spring of water. "Let us go and rest in the cool shade," said they. So they went and rested, and the old woman came out of the hut to them.--"Hast thou a daughter, little mother?" said they.--"Yes, that I have," said she.--"One or two?" they asked.--"Well, there is another," said she, "but she is not my daughter, she is a mere kitchen slut, the very look of her is nasty."--"Very well," said they, "we will measure them with the golden slippers."--"Good!" cried the old woman. Then she said to her own daughter, "Go, my dear little daughter, tidy thyself up a bit, and wash thy little feet!"--But the old man's daughter she drove behind the stove, and the poor thing was neither washed nor dressed. "Sit there, thou daughter of a dog!" said she.--Then the Tsar's councillors came into the hut to measure, and the old woman said to her daughter, "Put out thy little foot, darling!"--The councillors then measured with the slippers, but they wouldn't fit her at all. Then they said, "Tell us, little mother, where is thy other daughter?"-- "Oh, as for her, she is a mere slut, and besides she isn't dressed."--"No matter," said they; "where is she?"--Then she came out

THE TSAR'S COUNCILLORS WENT TO THE HOUSES OF ALL THE
NOBLES AND PRINCES

from behind the stove, and her stepmother hustled her and said, "Get along, thou sluttish hussy!"--Then they measured her with the slippers, and they fitted like gloves, whereupon the courtiers rejoiced exceedingly and praised the Lord.

"Well, little mother," said they, "we will take this daughter away with us."--"What! take a slattern like that? Why, all the people will laugh at you!"--"Maybe they will," said they.--Then the old woman scolded, and wouldn't let her go. "How can such a slut become the consort of the Tsar's son?" screeched she.--"Nay, but she must come!" said they; "go, dress thyself, maiden!"--"Wait but a moment," said she, "and I'll tire myself as is meet!"--Then she went to the spring beneath the willow-tree, and washed and dressed herself, and she came back so lovely and splendid that the like of it can neither be thought of nor guessed at, but only told of in tales. As she entered the hut she shone like the sun, and her stepmother had not another word to say.

So they put her in a carriage and drove off, and when the Tsarevich saw her, he could not contain himself. "Make haste, O my father!" cried he, "and give us thy blessing." So the Tsar blessed them, and they were wedded. Then they made a great feast and invited all the world to it. And they lived happily together, and ate wheat-bread to their hearts' content.

R. NISBET BAIN

THE IRON WOLF

THERE was once upon a time a parson who had a servant, and when this servant had served him faithfully for twelve years and upward, he came to the parson and said, "Let us now settle our accounts, master, and pay me what thou owest me. I have now served long enough, and would fain have a little place in the wide world all to myself."--"Good!" said the parson. "I'll tell thee now what wage I'll give thee for thy faithful service. I'll give thee this egg. Take it home, and when thou gettest there, make to thyself a cattle-pen, and make it strong; then break the egg in the middle of thy cattle-pen, and thou shalt see something. But whatever thou doest, don't break it on thy way home, or all thy luck will leave thee."

So the servant departed on his homeward way. He went on and on, and at last he thought to himself, "Come now, I'll see what is inside this egg of mine!" So he broke it, and out of it came all sorts of cattle in such numbers that the open steppe became like a fair. The servant stood there in amazement, and he thought to himself, "However in God's world shall I be able to drive all these cattle back again?" He had scarcely uttered the words when the Iron Wolf came running up, and said to him, "I'll collect and drive back all these cattle into the egg again, and I'll patch the egg up so that it will become quite whole. But in return for that," continued the Iron Wolf, "whenever thou dost sit down on the bridal bench,[17] I'll come and eat thee."--"Well," thought the servant to himself, "a lot of things may happen before I sit down on the bridal bench and he comes to eat me, and in the meantime I shall get all these cattle. Agreed, then," said he. So the Iron Wolf immediately collected all the cattle, and drove them back into the egg, and patched up the egg and made it whole just as it was before.

The servant went home to the village where he lived, made him a cattle-pen stronger than strong, went inside it and broke the egg, and immediately that cattle-pen was as full of cattle as it could hold. Then he took to farming and cattle-breeding, and he became so rich that in the whole wide world there was none richer than he. He kept to himself, and his goods increased and multiplied exceedingly; the only thing wanting to his happiness was a wife, but a wife he was afraid to take. Now near to where he lived was a General who had a lovely daughter, and this daughter fell in love with the rich man. So the General went and said to him, "Come, why don't you marry? I'll give you my daughter and lots of money with her."--"How is it possible for me to marry?" replied the man; "as soon as ever I sit down on the bridal bench, the Iron Wolf will come and eat me up." And he told the General all that had happened.--"Oh, nonsense!" said the General, "don't be afraid. I have a mighty host, and when the time comes for you to sit down on the bridal bench, we'll surround your house with three strong rows of soldiers, and *they* won't let the Iron Wolf get at you, I can tell you." So they talked the matter over till he let himself be persuaded, and then they began to make great preparations for the bridal banquet. Everything went off excellently well, and they made merry till the time came when bride and bridegroom were to sit down together on the bridal bench. Then the General placed his men in three strong rows all round the house so as not to let the Iron Wolf get in; and no sooner had the young people sat down upon the bridal bench, than, sure enough, the Iron Wolf came running up. He saw the host standing round the house in three strong rows, but through all three rows he leaped and made straight for the house. But the man, as soon as he saw the Iron Wolf, leaped out of the window, mounted his horse, and galloped off with the wolf after him.

Away and away he galloped, and after him came the wolf, but try as it would, it could not catch him up anyhow. At last, toward evening, the man stopped and looked about him, and saw that he was in a lone forest, and before him stood a hut. He went up to this hut, and saw an old man and an old woman sitting in front of it, and said to them, "Would you let me rest a little while with you, good people?"--"By all means!" said they.--"There is one thing, however, good people!" said he, "don't let the Iron Wolf catch me while I am resting with you."--"Have no fear of that!" replied the old couple. "We have a dog called Chutko,[18] who can hear a wolf coming a mile off, and he'll be sure to let us know." So he laid him down to sleep, and was just dropping off when Chutko began to bark. Then the old people awoke him, and said, "Be off! be off! for the Iron Wolf is coming." And they gave him the dog, and a wheaten hearth-cake as provision by the way.

So he went on and on, and the dog followed after him till it began to grow dark, and then he perceived another hut in another forest. He went up to that hut, and in front of it were sitting an old man and an old woman. He asked them for a night's lodging. "Only," said he, "take care that the Iron Wolf doesn't catch me!"--"Have no fear of that," said they. "We have a dog here called Vazhko,[19] who can hear a wolf nine miles off." So he laid him down and slept. Just before dawn Vazhko began to bark. Immediately they awoke him. "Run!" cried they, "the Iron Wolf is coming!" And they gave him the dog, and a barley hearth-cake as provision by the way. So he took the hearth-cake, sat him on his horse, and off he went, and his two dogs followed after him.

He went on and on. On and on he went till evening, when again he stopped and looked about him, and he saw that he was in another forest, and another little hut stood before him. He went into the hut, and there were sitting an old man and an old woman. "Will you let me pass the night here, good people?" said he; "only take care that the Iron Wolf does not get hold of me!"-- "Have no fear!" said they, "we have a dog called Bary, who can hear a wolf coming twelve miles off. He'll let us know." So he lay down to sleep, and early in the morning Bary let them know that the Iron Wolf was drawing nigh. Immediately they awoke him.

"'Tis high time for you to be off!" said they. Then they gave him the dog, and a buckwheat hearth-cake as provision by the way. He took the hearth-cake, sat him on his horse, and off he went. So now he had three dogs, and they all three followed him.

He went on and on, and toward evening he found himself in front of another hut. He went into it, and there was nobody there. He went and lay down, and his dogs lay down also, Chutko on the threshold of the room door, Vazhko at the threshold of the house door, and Bary at the threshold of the outer gate. Presently the Iron Wolf came trotting up. Immediately Chutko gave the alarm, Vazhko nailed him to the earth, and Bary tore him to pieces.

Then the man gathered his faithful dogs around him, mounted his horse, and went back to his own home.

THE THREE BROTHERS

THERE were, once upon a time, three brothers, and the third was a fool. And in their little garden grew golden apple-trees with golden apples, and not far off lived a hog that had taken a fancy to these apples. So the father sent his sons into the garden to guard the trees. The eldest went first, and sat and sat and watched and watched till he was tired of watching, and fell asleep. Then the hog crept in, and dug and dug till he had digged up an apple-tree, which he ate up, and then went his way. The father got up next morning and counted his apple-trees, and one of them was gone. The next night the father sent the second son to watch. He waited and watched till he also fell asleep, and the hog came again and dug up and ate another golden apple-tree and made off. The next morning the father got up again and counted his trees, and another was gone. Then the fool said, "Dad, let me go too!" But the father said, "Oh, fool, fool, wherefore shouldst thou go? Thy wise brethren have watched to no purpose, what canst thou do?"--"Hoity-toity!" said the fool; "give me a gun, and I'll go all the same." His father wouldn't give him a gun, so he took it, and went to watch. He placed his gun across his knees and sat down. He sat and sat, but nothing came, nothing came; he got drowsy, was nodding off, when his gun fell off his knees, and he awoke with a start and watched more warily. At last he heard something--and there stood the hog. It began to dig up another tree, when he pulled the trigger and--bang! His brothers heard the sound, came running up, were quite amazed to see a dead boar lying there, and said, "What will become of us now?"--"Let us kill him," said the eldest brother, "and bury him in that ditch, and say that we killed the hog." So they took and slew him, and buried him in the ditch, and took the hog to their father, and said,

"While we were watching, this hog came up and began digging, so we killed him and have brought him to you."

One day a nobleman came by that way, and was surprised to see a beautiful elder-bush growing out of the ditch; so he went up to it, cut off a branch, made him a flute out of it, and began playing upon it. But the flute played of its own accord, and made this moan:

> *"Play, good master, play,*
> *But steal not my heart away!*
> *Me my brothers took and slew,*
> *In the ditch my body threw,*
> *For that hog shot down by me*
> *That rooted up the tree."*

The nobleman then went on to the inn, and there he found the fool's father. "Such a funny thing has happened to me," said the nobleman. "I went and cut me out a flute from an elder-bush, and lo! it plays of its own accord!" Then the father took the flute and tried his hand at it, and it sang:

> *"Play, good daddy, play,*
> *But don't steal my heart away!*
> *Me my brothers took and slew,*
> *In the ditch my body threw,*
> *For that hog shot down by me,*
> *That rooted up the tree!"*

The father was so astonished that he bought it, and took it home, and gave it to the mother for her to play upon it, and it sang:

> *"Play, good mammy, play,*
> *But don't steal my heart away!*
> *Me my brothers took and slew,*
> *In the ditch my body threw,*
> *For that hog shot down by me,*
> *That rooted up the tree!"*

Then the father gave the flute to his brothers to play upon, but they wouldn't. "Nay, but you must!" said their father. Then the younger brother took and played upon it:

> *"Play, my brother, play,*
> *But don't steal my heart away!*
> *Me my brothers took and slew,*
> *In the ditch my body threw,*
> *For the hog shot down by me,*
> *That rooted up the tree!"*

Then the father gave the flute to the elder brother who had slain him, but he wouldn't take it. "Take it and play upon it!" roared his father at him. Then he took it and played:

> *"Play, my brother, play,*
> *But don't steal my heart away!*
> *'Twas thou who didst me slay,*
> *And stowed my corpse away,*
> *For the hog shot down by me,*
> *That rooted up the tree!"*

"Then it was thou who didst slay him?" cried the father. What could the elder brother do but confess it! Then they dug the dead man up, and buried him in the cemetery; but they tied the elder brother to a wild horse, which scattered his bones about the endless steppe.

But I was there, and drank wine and mead till my beard was wet.

THE TSAR AND THE ANGEL

SOMEWHERE, nowhere, in a certain kingdom, in a certain empire, time out of mind, and in no land of ours, dwelt a Tsar who was so proud, so very proud, that he feared neither God nor man. He listened to no good counsel from whithersoever it might come, but did only that which was good in his own eyes, and nobody durst put him right. And all his ministers and nobles grieved exceedingly, and all the people grieved likewise.

One day this Tsar went to church; the priest was reading from Holy Scripture, and so he needs must listen. Now there were certain words there which pleased him not. "To say such words to me!" thought he, "words that I can never forget, though I grow grey-headed." After service the Tsar went home, and bade them send the priest to him. The priest came. "How durst thou read such and such passages to me?" said the Tsar.--"They were written to be read," replied the priest.--"Written, indeed! And wouldst thou then read everything that is written? Smear those places over with grease, and never dare to read them again, I say!"--"'Tis not I who have written those words, your Majesty," said the priest; "nor is it for such as I to smear them over."--"What! thou dost presume to teach me? I am the Tsar, and it is thy duty to obey me."--"In all things will I obey thee, O Tsar, save only in sacred things. God is over them, men cannot alter them."--"Not alter them!" roared the Tsar; "if I wish them altered, altered they must be. Strike me out those words instantly, I say, and never dare read them in church again. Dost hear?"--"I dare not," said the priest, "I have no will in the matter."--"I command thee, fellow!"--"I dare not, O Tsar!"--"Well," said the Tsar, "I'll give thee three days to think about it, and on the evening of the fourth

109

day appear before me, and I'll strike thy head from thy shoulders if thou dost not obey me!" Then the priest bowed low and went home.

The third day was already drawing to a close, and the priest knew not what to do. It was no great terror to him to die for the faith, but what would become of his wife and children? He walked about, and wept, and wrung his hands: "Oh, woe is me! woe is me!" At last he lay down on his bed, but sleep he could not. Only toward dawn did he doze off, then he saw in a dream an angel standing at his head. "Fear nothing!" said the angel. "God hath sent me down on earth to protect thee!" So, early in the morning, the priest rose up full of joy and prayed gratefully to God.

The Tsar also awoke early in the morning, and bawled to his huntsmen to gather together and go a-hunting with him in the forest.

So away they went hunting in the forest, and it was not long before a stag leaped out of the thicket beneath the very eyes of the Tsar. Off after it went the Tsar; every moment the stag seemed to be faltering, and yet the Tsar could never quite come up with it. Hot with excitement, the Tsar spurred his horse on yet faster. "Gee up! gee up!" he cried; "now we've got him!" But here a stream crossed the road, and the stag plunged into the water. The Tsar was a good swimmer. "I've got him now, at any rate," thought he. "A little longer, and I shall hold him by the horns." So the Tsar took off his clothes, and into the water he plunged after the stag. But the stag swam across to the opposite bank, and the Tsar was extending his hand to seize him by the horns––when there was no longer any stag to be seen. It was the angel who had taken the form of a stag. The Tsar was amazed. He looked about him on every side, and wondered where the stag had gone. Then he saw someone on the other side of the river putting on his clothes, and presently the man mounted his horse and galloped away. The Tsar thought it was some evil-doer, but it was the self-same angel that had now put on the Tsar's clothes and gone away to collect the huntsmen and take them home. As for the Tsar, he remained all naked and solitary in the forest.

At last he looked about him and saw, far, far away, smoke rising above the forest, and something like a dark cloud standing in the clear sky. "Maybe," thought he, "that is my hunting-pavilion." So he went in the direction of the smoke, and came at last to a brick-kiln. The brick-burners came forth to meet him, and were amazed to see a naked man. "What is he doing here?" they thought. And they saw that his feet were lame and bruised, and his body covered with scratches. "Give me to drink," said he, "and I would fain eat something also." The brick-burners had pity on him; they gave him an old tattered garment to wear and a piece of black bread and a gherkin to eat. Never from the day of his birth had the Tsar had such a tasty meal. "And now speak, O man!" said they; "who art thou?"--"I'll tell you who I am," said he, when he had eaten his fill; "I am your Tsar. Lead me to my capital, and there I will reward you!"--"What, thou wretched rogue!" they cried, "thou dost presume to mock us, thou old ragamuffin, and magnify thyself into a Tsar! Thou reward us, indeed!" And they looked at him in amazement and scorn.--"Dare to laugh at me again," said he, "and I'll have your heads chopped off!" For he forgot himself, and thought he was at home.--"What! thou!" Then they fell upon him and beat him. They beat him and hauled him about most unmercifully, and then they drove him away, and off he went bellowing through the forest.

He went on and on till at last he saw once more a smoke rising up out of the wood. Again he thought, "That is surely my hunting-pavilion," and so he went up to it. And toward evening he came to another brick-kiln. There, too, they had pity upon and kindly entreated him. They gave him to eat and to drink. They also gave him ragged hose and a tattered shirt, for they were very poor people. They took him to be a runaway soldier, or some other poor man, but when he had eaten his fill and clothed himself, he said to them, "I am your Tsar!" They laughed at him, and again he began to talk roughly to the people. Then they fell upon him and thrashed him soundly, and drove him right away. And he wandered all by himself through the forest till it was night. Then he laid him down beneath a tree, and so he passed the night, and rising up very early, fared on his way straight before him.

At last he came to a third brick-kiln, but he did not tell the brick-burners there that he was the Tsar. All he thought of now was how he might reach his capital. The people here, too, treated him kindly, and seeing that his feet were lame and bruised, they had compassion upon him, and gave him a pair of very, very old boots. And he asked them, "Do ye know by which way I can get to the capital?" They told him, but it was a long, long journey that would take the whole day.

So he went the way they had told him, and he went on and on till he came to a little town, and there the roadside sentries stopped him. "Halt!" they cried. He halted. "Your passport!"[20]--"I have none."--"What! no passport? Then thou art a vagabond. Seize him!" they cried. So they seized him and put him in a dungeon. Shortly after they came to examine him, and asked him, "Whence art thou?"--"From such and such a capital," said he. Then they ordered him to be put in irons and taken thither.

So they took him back to that capital and put him in another dungeon. Then the custodians came round to examine the prisoners, and one said one thing and one said another, till at last it came to the turn of the Tsar.--"Who art thou, old man?" they asked. Then he told them the whole truth. "Once I was the Tsar," said he, and he related all that had befallen him. Then they were much amazed, for he was not at all like a Tsar. For indeed he had been growing thin and haggard for a long time, and his beard was all long and tangled. And yet, for all that, he stood them out that he was the Tsar. So they made up their minds that he was crazy, and drove him away. "Why should we keep this fool forever," said they, "and waste the Tsar's bread upon him?" So they let him go, and never did any man feel so wretched on God's earth as did that wretched Tsar. Willingly would he have done any sort of work if he had only known how, but he had never been used to work, so he had to go along begging his bread, and could scarce beg enough to keep body and soul together. He lay at night at the first place that came to hand, sometimes in the tall grass of the steppes, sometimes beneath a fence. "That it should ever have come to this!" he sighed.

But the angel who had made himself Tsar went home with the huntsmen. And no man knew that he was not a Tsar, but an angel. The same evening that priest came to him and said, "Do thy will, O Tsar, and strike off my head, for I cannot blot out one word of Holy Scripture."--And the Tsar said to him, "Glory be to God, for now I know that there is at least one priest in my tsardom who stands firm for God's Word. I'll make thee the highest bishop in this realm." The priest thanked him, bowed down to the earth, and departed marvelling. "What is this wonder?" thought he, "that the haughty Tsar should have become so just and gentle."--But all men marvelled at the change that had come over the Tsar. He was now so mild and gracious, nor did he spend all his days in the forest, but went about inquiring of his people if any were wronged or injured by their neighbours, and if justice were done. He took count of all, and rebuked the unjust judges, and saw that every man had his rights. And the people now rejoiced as much as they had grieved heretofore, and justice was done in all the tribunals, and no bribes were taken.

But the Tsar, the real Tsar, grew more and more wretched. Then, after three years, a ukase went forth that on such and such a day all the people were to come together to a great banquet given by the Tsar, all were to be there, both rich and poor, both high and lowly. And all the people came, and the unhappy Tsar came too. And so many long tables were set out in the Tsar's courtyard that all the people praised God when they saw the glad sight. And they all sat down at table and ate and drank, and the Tsar himself and his courtiers distributed the meat and drink to the guests as much as they would, but to the unfortunate Tsar they gave a double portion of everything. And they all ate and drank their fill,

113

THE TSAR WENT ABOUT INQUIRING OF HIS PEOPLE IF ANY
WERE WRONGED

and then the Tsar began to inquire of the people whether any had suffered wrong or had not had justice done him.

And when the people began to disperse, the Tsar stood at the gate with a bag of money, and gave to everyone a *grivna*,[21] but to the unhappy Tsar he gave three.

And after three years the Tsar gave another banquet, and again entertained all the people. And when he had given them both to eat and to drink as much as they would, he inquired of them what was being done in his tsardom, and again gave a *grivna* to each one of them; but to the unlucky Tsar he gave a double portion of meat and drink and three *grivni*.

And again, after three years, he made yet another banquet, and proclaimed that all should come, both rich and poor, both earls and churls. And all the people came and ate and drank and bowed low before the Tsar and thanked him, and made ready to depart. The unlucky Tsar was also on the point of going, when the angel Tsar stopped him, and took him aside into the palace, and said to him, "Lo! God hath tried thee and chastised thy pride these ten years. But me He sent to teach thee that a Tsar must have regard to the complaints of his people. So thou wast made poor and a vagabond on the face of the earth that thou mightst pick up wisdom, if but a little. Look now, that thou doest good to thy people, and judgest righteous judgment, as from henceforth thou shalt be Tsar again, but I must fly back to God in heaven."-- And when he had said this he bade them wash and shave him (for his beard had grown right down to his girdle), and put upon him the raiment of a Tsar. And the angel said further, "Go now into the inner apartments. There the courtiers of the Tsar are sitting and making merry, and none will recognize in thee the vagabond old man. May God help thee always to do good!" And when the angel had said this he was no more to be seen, and only his clothes remained on the floor.

Then the Tsar prayed gratefully to God, and went to the merry-making of his courtiers, and henceforth he ruled his people justly, as the angel had bidden him.

THE STORY OF IVAN AND THE DAUGHTER OF THE SUN

THERE were once upon a time four brethren, and three of them remained at home, while the fourth went out to seek for work. This youngest brother came to a strange land, and hired himself out to a husbandman for three gold pieces a year. For three years he served his master faithfully, so, at the end of his time, he departed with nine gold pieces in his pocket. The first thing he now did was to go to a spring, and into this spring he threw three of his gold pieces. "Let us see now," said he, "if I have been honest, they will come swimming back to me." Then he lay down by the side of the spring and went fast asleep. How long he slept there, who can tell? but at any rate he woke up at last and went to the spring, but there was no sign of his money to be seen. Then he threw three more of the gold pieces into the spring, and again he lay down by the side of it and slept. Then he got up and went and looked into the spring, and still there was no sign of the money. So he threw in his three remaining gold pieces, and again lay down and slept. The third time he arose and looked into the spring, and there, sure enough, was his money: all nine of the gold pieces were floating on the surface of the water!

And now his heart felt lighter, and he gathered up the nine gold pieces and went on his way. On the road he fell in with three *katsapi*[22] with a laden wagon. He asked them concerning their wares, and they said they were carrying a load of incense. He begged them straightway to sell him this incense. Then they sold it to him for the gold pieces, and when he had bought it and they had departed, he kindled fire and burnt the incense, and offered it up to God as a sweet-smelling sacrifice. Then an angel flew down

117

to him, and said, "Oh, thou that hast offered this sweet-smelling sacrifice to God, what dost thou want for thine own self? Dost thou want a tsardom, or great riches? Or, perchance, the desire of thy heart is a good wife? Speak, for God will give thee whatsoever thou desirest." When the man had listened to the angel, he said to him, "Tarry a while! I will go and ask those people who are ploughing yonder." Now those people who were ploughing there were his own brethren, but he did not know that they were his brethren. So he went up and said to the elder brother, "Tell me, uncle, what shall I ask of God? A tsardom, or great riches, or a good wife? Tell me, which of the three is the best gift to ask for?"--And his eldest brother said to him, "I know not, and who does know? Go and ask someone else." So he went to the second brother, who was ploughing a little farther on. He asked him the same question, but the man only shrugged his shoulders and said he didn't know either. Then he went to the third brother, who was the youngest of the three, and also ploughing there. And he asked him, saying, "Tell me, now, which is the best gift to ask of God: a tsardom, or great riches, or a good wife?"--And the third brother said, "What a question! Thou art too young for a tsardom, and great riches last but for a little while; ask God for a good wife, for if it please God to give thee a good wife, 'tis a gift that will bless thee all thy life long." So he went back to the angel and asked for a good wife. Then he went on his way till he came to a certain wood, and, looking about him, he perceived that in this wood was a lake. And while he was looking at it, three wild doves came flying along and lit down upon this lake. They threw off their plumage and plunged into the water, and then he saw that they were not wild doves, but three fair ladies. They bathed in the lake, and in the meantime the youth crept up and took the raiment of one of them and hid it behind the bushes. When they came out of the water the third lady missed her clothes. Then the youth said to her, "I know where thy clothes are, but I will not give them to thee unless thou wilt be my wife."--"Good!" cried she, "thy wife will I be." Then she dressed herself, and they went together to the nearest village. When they got there, she said to him, "Now go to

118

the nobleman who owns the land here, and beg him for a place where we may build us a hut." So he went right up to the nobleman's castle and entered his reception-room, and said, "Glory be to God!"--"Forever and ever!" replied the nobleman. "What dost thou want here, Ivan?"--"I have come, sir, to beg of thee a place where I may build me a hut."--"A place for a hut, eh? Good, very good. Go home, and I'll speak to my overseer, and he shall appoint thee a place."--So he returned from the nobleman's castle, and his wife said to him, "Go now into the forest and cut down an oak, a young oak, that thou canst span round with both arms." So he cut down such an oak as his wife had told him of, and she built a hut of the oak, for the overseer had come and shown them a place where they might build their hut. But when the overseer returned home he praised loudly to his master the wife of this Ivan. "She is such and such," said he. "Fair she may be," replied the nobleman, "but she is another's."--"She need not be another's for long," replied the overseer. "This Ivan is in our hands; let us send him to see why it is the sun grows so red when he sets."--"That's just the same as if you sent him to a place whence he can never return."--"All the better."--Then they sent for Ivan, and gave him this errand, and he returned home to his wife, weeping bitterly. Then his wife asked him all about it, and said, "Well, I can tell thee all about the ways of the sun, for I am the sun's own daughter. So now I'll tell thee the whole matter. Go back to this nobleman and say to him that the reason why the sun turns so red as he sets is this: Just as the sun is going down into the sea, three fair ladies rise out of it, and it is the sight of them which makes him turn so red all over!" So he went back and told them. "Oh-ho!" cried they, "if you can go as far as that, you may now go a little farther"; so they told him to go to hell and see how it was there. "Yes," said his wife, "I know the road that leads to hell also very well; but the nobleman must let his overseer go with thee, or else he never will believe that thou really didst go to hell."--So the nobleman told his overseer that he must go to hell too, so they went together; and when they got there the rulers of hell laid hands upon the overseer straightway. "Thou dog!"

119

roared they, "we've been looking out for thee for some time!" So Ivan returned without the overseer, and the nobleman said to him, "Where's my overseer?"--"I left him in hell," said Ivan, "and they said there that they were waiting for you, sir, too." When the nobleman heard this he hanged himself, but Ivan lived happily with his wife.

THE RULERS OF HELL LAID HANDS UPON THE OVERSEER
STRAIGHTWAY

THE CAT, THE COCK, AND THE FOX

THERE was once upon a time a cat and a cock, who agreed to live together, so they built them a hut on an ash-heap, and the cock kept house while the cat went foraging for sausages.

One day the fox came running up: "Open the door, little cock!" cried she.--"Pussy told me not to, little fox!" said the cock.-- "Open the door, little cock!" repeated the fox.--"I tell you, pussy told me not to, little fox!"--At last, however, the cock grew tired of always saying "No!" so he opened the door, and in the fox rushed, seized him in her jaws, and ran off with him. Then the cock cried:

> *"Help! pussy-pussy!*
> *That foxy hussy*
> *Has got me tight*
> *With all her might.*
> *Across her tail*
> *My legs do trail*
> *Along the bridge so stony!"*

The cat heard it, gave chase to the fox, rescued the cock, brought him home, scolded him well, and said, "Now keep out of her jaws in the future, if you don't want to be killed altogether!"

Then the cat went out foraging for wheat, so that the cock might have something to eat. He had scarcely gone when the sly she-fox again came creeping up. "Dear little cock!" said she, "pray open the door!"--"Nay, little fox! Pussy said I wasn't to." But the fox went on asking and asking till at last the cock let him in.

Then the fox rushed at him, seized him by the neck, and ran off with him. Then the cock cried out:

> "Help! pussy-pussy!
> That foxy hussy
> Has got me tight
> With all her might.
> Across her tail
> My legs do trail
> Along the bridge so stony!"

The cat heard it, and again he ran after the fox and rescued the cock, and gave the fox a sound drubbing. Then he said to the cock, "Now, mind you never let her come in again, or she'll eat you."

But the next time the cat went out, the she-fox came again, and said, "Dear little cock, open the door!"--"No, little fox! Pussy said I wasn't to." But the fox begged and begged so piteously that, at last, the cock was quite touched, and opened the door. Then the fox caught him by the throat again, and ran away with him, and the cock cried:

> "Help! pussy-pussy!
> That foxy hussy
> Has got me tight
> With all her might.
> Across her tail
> My legs do trail
> Along the bridge so stony!"

The cat heard it, and gave chase again. He ran and ran, but this time he couldn't catch the fox up; so he returned home and wept bitterly, because he was now all alone. At last, however, he dried his tears and got him a little fiddle, a little fiddle-bow, and a big sack, and went to the fox's hole and began to play:

> *"Fiddle-de-dee!*
> *The foxy so wee*
> *Had daughters twice two,*
> *And a little son too,*
> *Called Phil.--Fiddle-dee!*
> *Come, foxy, and see*
> *My sweet minstrelsy!"*

Then the fox's daughter said, "Mammy, I'll go out and see who it is that is playing so nicely!" So out she skipped, but no sooner did pussy see her than he caught hold of her and popped her into his sack. Then he played again:

> *"Fiddle-de-dee!*
> *The foxy so wee*
> *Had daughters twice two,*
> *And a little son too,*
> *Called Phil.--Fiddle-dee!*
> *Come, foxy, and see*
> *My sweet minstrelsy!"*

Then the second daughter skipped out, and pussy caught her by the forehead, and popped her into his sack, and went on playing and singing till he had got all four daughters into his sack, and the little son also.

Then the old fox was left all alone, and she waited and waited, but not one of them came back. At last she said to herself, "I'll go out and call them home, for the cock is roasting, and the milk pottage is simmering, and 'tis high time we had something to eat." So out she popped, and the cat pounced upon her, and killed her too. Then he went and drank up all the soup, and gobbled up all the pottage, and then he saw the cock lying on a plate. "Come, shake yourself, cock!" said puss. So the cock shook himself, and got up, and the cat took the cock home, and the dead foxes too.

And when they got home they skinned them to make nice beds to lie upon, and lived happily together in peace and plenty. And as they laughed over the joke as a good joke, we may laugh over it too!

THE SERPENT-TSAREVICH
AND HIS TWO WIVES

THERE was once a Tsaritsa who had no child, and greatly desired one, so the soothsayers said to her, "Bid them catch thee a pike, bid them boil its head and nothing but its head, eat it, and thou shalt see what will happen." So she did so. She ate the pike's head and went about as usual for a whole year, and when the year was out she gave birth to a son who was a serpent.

And no sooner was he born than he looked about him, and said, "Mammy and daddy! Bid them make me a stone hut, and let there be a little bed there, and a little stove and a fire to warm me, and let me be married in a fortnight!"—So they did as he desired. They shut him up in a stone hut, with a little bed and a little stove and fire to warm him, and in a fortnight he grew quite big, indeed he grew too big for his little bed. "And now," said he, "I want to be married!" So they brought to him all the fair young damsels of the land that he might choose one to be his own true bride. Exceeding fair were all the damsels they brought him, and yet he would choose none of them. Now there was an old woman there, who had twelve daughters, and eleven of these daughters they brought to the Serpent-Tsarevich, but not the twelfth. "She is too young!" said they.—Then the youngest daughter said, "Ye fools, not to take me too! Why, if I were brought to the Serpent-Tsarevich, he would make me his bride at once."

Now this came to the Tsar's ears, and he commanded them to bring her to him straightway. And the Tsar said to her, "Wilt thou be my son's bride or not?"—And she said, "I will; but before I go to thy son, give me at once a score of chemises, and a score of

NINETEEN TIMES DID SHE CAST OFF ONE OF HER SUITS OF
CLOTHES

linen kirtles, and a score of woollen kirtles, and twenty pairs of shoes--twenty of each, I say."--So the Tsar gave them to her, and she put on the twenty chemises, the twenty linen kirtles, the twenty woollen kirtles, and the twenty pairs of shoes, one after the other, and went to see the Serpent-Tsarevich. When she came to the threshold of his hut, she stopped and said, "Hail, O Serpent-Tsarevich!"--"Hail, maiden!" cried he. "Wilt thou be my bride?"--"I will!"--"Then take off one of thy skins!" cried he.-- "Yes," she said, "but thou must do the same."--So he cast off one of his skins, and she cast off one of her twenty suits of clothes. Then he cried out again, "Cast off another of thy skins, maiden."- -"Yes," she replied, "but thou must cast off one too!"--So he did so. Nineteen times did he cast off one of his serpent's skins, and nineteen times did she cast off one of her suits of clothes, till at last she had only her every-day suit left, and he had only his human skin left. Then he threw off his last skin also, and it flew about in the air like a gossamer, whereupon she seized hold of it and threw it into the fire that was burning on the hearth till it was all consumed, and he stood before her no longer a serpent, but a simple Tsarevich. Then they married and lived happily together, but the husband never would go to visit his old father the Tsar, nor would he allow his bride to go near the palace.

The old Tsar sent for him again and again, but his son would never go. At last the wife was ashamed, and said to her husband one day, "Dear heart! let me go to thy father! I will only go for my own pastime, lest he get angry. Why should I not go?" Then he let her go, and she went to the court of the old Tsar, and took her pastime there. She amused herself finely, and ate and drank her fill of all good things. Now her husband had laid this command upon her, "Go and divert thyself if thou wilt, but if thou tell my father and my mother what has happened to me, and how I have lost my twenty serpent skins, thou shalt never see me more." For they did not know that he was now no longer a serpent, but a simple Tsarevich.

She vowed she would never tell; but for all her promises, she nevertheless told them at last how her husband had lost his twenty serpent skins. Then she enjoyed herself to her heart's content, but when she returned home she found no trace of her husband—he had departed to another kingdom in the uttermost parts of the world.

Then the poor bride sat her down and wept and wept, and when she had no more tears to weep, she went forth into the wide world to seek her husband. She went on till she came to a lonely little house, and she went and begged a night's lodging from the old woman who dwelt there, who was the Mother of the Winds. But the Mother of the Winds would not let her in. "God preserve thee, child!" said she. "My son is already winging his way hither. In another moment thou wilt hear the rustling of his wings, in another moment he will slay thee, and scatter thy bones to the four winds." But the bride besought the old woman till she had her desire, and the old woman hid her behind a huge chest. A moment afterward the son of the Mother of the Winds came flying up, and he smelt out the bride, and said, "What's this, mother? There is an evil smell of Cossack bones about the house!"—"No, it is not that," said his mother, "but a young woman has taken shelter here, who says that she is going in search of her husband."—"Then, mother, give her the little silver apple, and let her go, for her husband is in another kingdom." So they sent her away with the little silver apple.

She went on and on till night descended upon her, and she came to the lonely abode of another old woman, and begged a night's lodging of her also. But the old woman would not let her in. "My son will be here presently," said she, "and he will slay thee."—"Nay, but, granny," said the bride, "I've already stayed the night with such as thou, for I have lodged at the house of the Mother of the Winds."—Then the old woman took her in, and hid her, for she was the Mother of the Moon. And immediately afterward the Moon came flying up. "What is this, little mother?" cried he. "I smell an evil smell of Cossack bones!"—But she said to him,

"Nay, my dear little son, but a young woman has come hither who is obliged to search for her husband because she told his father and mother the truth." Then the Moon said, "'Twould be as well to let her go on farther. Give her the little golden apple, and let her be off as quickly as possible, for her husband is about to marry another wife." So she passed the night there, and in the morning they sent her away with the little golden apple.

She went on and on. Night again descended upon her, and she came to the house of the Mother of the Sun, and begged her for a night's lodging. But the old woman said to her, "I cannot let thee in. My son is flying about the world, but he will fly hither presently, and if he find thee here he will slay thee!"--Then the bride said, "Nay, but, granny dear, I have already lodged with the like of thee. I have lodged with the Mother of the Winds, and the Mother of the Moon, and they each gave me a little apple." Then the Mother of the Sun also let her in. Immediately afterward her son, the Sun, came flying up, and he said, "Why, what is this, little mother? I smell an evil smell of Cossack bones!"--But his mother answered, "A young woman came hither who begged for a night's lodging." She did not tell her son the whole truth, that the bride was in search of her husband, but he knew it already, and said, "Her husband is about to marry another wife. Let her go to the land where now he is, and give her the diamond apple, which is the best and most precious apple in the whole world, and tell her to hasten on to the house where her husband abides. They won't let her in there, but she must disguise herself as an old woman, and sit down outside in the courtyard, and spread out a cloth and lay upon it her little silver apple, and all the people will come flocking around to see the old woman who is selling apples of silver." So the bride did as the Sun bade her, and went to that distant empire, and the Empress of that empire, whom her husband had married, came to see what she was selling, and said to her, "What dost thou want for thy silver apple?" And she answered, "No money do I want for it. Oh, sovereign lady, all that I require in exchange therefor is that I may pass the night near my husband."--Then the Empress took the apple, and allowed her to come into the bedchamber of the Tsarevich to pass the night there; but first of all she gave the Tsarevich a sleeping draught so that he knew nothing, and could speak not a word to her, nor could he even recognize what manner of person his true wife was. Then only did the Empress let her come into the room where her husband lay. And she watched over him, she watched over him the live-long night, and with the dawn she departed.

The next morning he awoke out of his drugged sleep, and said to himself, "Why, what is this? It is just as if my first wife has been weeping over me here, and wetted me with her tears!" But he told nobody what he thought, nor did he say a word about it to his second wife. "Wait a bit!" thought he, "to-morrow night I'll not go to sleep. I'll watch and watch till I watch the thing out."

The next day the faithful wife spread out her little cloth again, and laid upon it her golden apple. The Empress again came that way, went up to her, and said, "Sell me that apple of thine, and I'll give thee for it as many pence as thou canst hold in thy lap!"--But she replied, "Nay, my sovereign lady! money for it I will not take, but let me pass one more night in my own husband's room!"--And the Empress took the apple, and let her go there. But first the Empress caressed and kissed her husband into a good humour, and then she gave him another sleeping draught. And the faithful wife came again, and watched and wept over him and wetted him with her tears, and with the dawn she departed.

And now she had only one apple left, but that was the diamond apple, the most precious apple in the world. And she said to the Empress, "Let me watch by him for this apple but one night more, and I'll never ask again!" And she let her. Now this night also her husband was asleep. And his first wife came and immediately began to kiss him on the head, but he said nothing. Then she kissed him again, and at last he awoke and started up, and said, "Who's that?"--"It is I, thy first wife."--"How hast thou found thy way hither?"--"Oh, I have been here and there and everywhere. I have lodged with the Mother of the Winds, and the Mother of the Moon, and the Mother of the Sun, and they gave me three apples, and I gave these apples to thy Empress-wife, and she let me watch over thee, and this is the third night that I have watched by thy side."

Then he came to his right mind, and cried aloud that they should bring in lights, and he saw that his faithful wife was quite an old woman. Then he bethought him, and said, "Was ever the like of this known? My first and faithful wife goes a-seeking her husband throughout the wide world, while my accursed second wife, Empress though she be, sells her husband for three apples!"

Then he bade them give his faithful wife rich garments as much as she would, and she stripped off her disguise, and washed her face and grew young again. But the faithless wife was tied to the tails of four wild horses, and they tore her to pieces in the endless steppe.

R. Nisbet Bain

THE ORIGIN OF THE MOLE

ONCE upon a time a rich man and a poor man had a field in common, and they sowed it with the same seed at the same time. But God prospered the poor man's labour and made his seed to grow, but the rich man's seed did not grow. Then the rich man claimed that part of the field where the grain had sprung up, and said to the poor man, "Look now! 'tis my seed that has prospered, and not thine!" The poor man protested, but the rich man would not listen, but said to him, "If thou wilt not believe me, then, poor man, come into the field quite early to-morrow morning, before dawn, and God shall judge betwixt us."

Then the poor man went home. But the rich man dug a deep trench in the poor man's part of the field and placed his son in it, and said to him, "Look now, my son; when I come hither to-morrow morning and ask whose field this is, say that it is not the poor man's, but the rich man's."

Then he well covered up his son with straw, and departed to his own house.

In the morning all the people assembled together and went to the field, and the rich man cried, "Speak, O God! whose field is this, the rich man's or the poor man's?"

"The rich man's, the rich man's," cried a voice from the midst of the field.

But the Lord Himself was among the people gathered together there, and He said, "Listen not to that voice, for the field is verily the poor man's."

Then the Lord told all the people how the matter went, and then He said to the son of the rich man,

"Stay where thou art, and sit beneath the earth all thy days, so long as the sun is in the sky."

So the rich man's son became a mole on the spot, and that is why the mole always flies the light of day.

THE TWO PRINCES

THERE was once upon a time a King who had two sons, and these sons went a-hunting in the forest and there lost themselves. They wandered on and on for twelve weeks, and at the end of the twelve weeks they came to a place where three roads met, and the elder brother said to the younger, "My brother, here our roads part. Take thou the road on that side, and I'll take the road on this." Then the elder brother took a knife and stuck it into the trunk of a maple-tree by the roadside, and said, "Look now, brother, should any blood drip from the blade of this knife it will be a sign that I am perishing, and thou must go and seek me; but if any blood flow from the handle, it will be a sign that *thou* art perishing, and I will then go and seek thee." Then the brothers embraced each other and parted, and one went in one direction and the other went in the other.

The elder brother went on and on and on till he came to a mountain so high that there cannot be a higher, and he began climbing it with his dog and his stick. He went on till he came to an apple-tree, and beneath the apple-tree a fire was burning, and he stopped to warm himself, when an old woman came up and said to him, "Dear little gentleman! dear little gentleman! tie up that dog lest he bite me." So he took the dog and tied it up, and immediately he was turned to stone, and the dog too, for the old woman was a pagan witch.

Time passed, and the younger brother came back to the maple-tree by the cross-roads and saw that blood was dripping from the blade of the knife. Then he knew that his brother was perishing, and he went in search of him, and came at last to the high mountain that was higher than all others, and on the top of this mountain there was a little courtyard, and in the courtyard an old woman, who said to him, "Little Prince, what brings thee hither, and what dost thou seek?"--"I seek my brother," said he; "a whole year has passed since I heard of him, and I know not whether he be alive or dead."--Then she said to him, "I can tell thee that he is dead, and it is of no use seeking for him, though thou goest the wide world over. But go up that mountain, and thou wilt come to two other mountains opposite to each other, and there thou wilt find an old man, who will put thee on thy way." So he went up the high mountain till he came to two other mountains that were opposite each other, and there he saw two old men sitting, and they asked him straightway, "Little Prince! little Prince! whither dost thou go, and what dost thou seek?"--"I am going in search of my brother," said he, "my dear elder brother who is perishing, and I can find him nowhere."--Then one of the old men said to him, "If thou canst scale those two mountains yonder without falling, I'll give thee all that thou dost want." Then he scaled the two mountains as nimbly as a goat, and the old man gave him a bast rope, three fathoms long, and bade him return to the mountain where was the fire and the old woman who had asked him to stay and warm himself, and bind this old woman with the cord and beat her till she promised to bring his brother back to life again, and not only his brother but a Tsar and a Tsaritsa[23] and a Tsarivna, who were also turned to stone there. "Beat her till she has brought them all to life again," said they. So he took the cord and went back to where the fire was burning. An apple-tree was there, and beneath the apple-tree was the fire, and the old witch came out to him and said, "Little master! little master! let me come and warm myself."--"Come along, little mother!" cried he; "come and warm thyself and make thyself comfortable." Then she came out, but no sooner had she done so, than he threw the cord around her and began flogging her. "Say," cried he, "what hast thou done with my brother?"--"Oh, dear little master! dear little master! let me go, let me go! I'll tell thee this instant where thy brother is." But he wouldn't listen, but beat her and beat her, and held her naked feet over the fire, and toasted and roasted her till she shrivelled right up. Then he let her go, and she went with him to a cave that was on that mountain, and drew from the depths of it some healing and life-giving water, and brought his brother back to life again, but it was as much as she could do, for she was half dead herself. Then his brother said to him, "Oh, my dear brother, how heavily I must have been sleeping! But thou must revive my faithful dog too!" Then she revived the faithful dog, and she also revived the Tsar and the Tsaritsa and the Tsarivna, who had been turned to stone there. Then they left that place and when they had gone a little distance, the elder brother bowed to the ground and went on his way alone.

He went on and on till he came to a city where all the people were weeping and all the houses were hung with black cloth. And he said to them, "Why do ye weep, and why are all your houses hung with black?"--And they answered, "Because there's a Dragon here who eats the people, and it has come to such a pass with us that to-morrow we must give him our Princess for dinner."--"Nay, but ye shall not do this thing," said he, and, with that, he set out for the cavern where the Dragon lived, and tethered his horse there and slept by the side of the cavern all night. And the next day, sure enough, the Princess was brought to the mouth of the cavern. She came driving thither in a carriage and four and with a heyduck[24] in attendance. But when the Prince saw her, he came forth to meet her and led her aside and gave her a prayer-book in her hand, and said to her, "Stay here, Princess, and pray to God for me." Then she fell down on her knees and began to pray, and the Dragon popped one of his heads out of the cavern and said, "It is time I had my dinner now, and there's not so much as a breakfast here!" But the Prince also fell down on his knees and read out of his prayer-book and prayed to God, and said to the Dragon, "Come forth! come forth! and I'll give thee breakfast and dinner at the same time!" Then the Dragon darted back again, but when he had waited till midday and still there was neither breakfast nor dinner for him, he popped two of his heads out and cried, "It is high time I had my dinner, and still there is neither breakfast nor dinner for me!"--"Come forth, and I'll give thee both at once!" cried the Prince. Then the Dragon wouldn't wait any longer, but stuck out all his six heads and began to wriggle out of the cavern; but the Prince attacked him with his huge broadsword, a full fathom long, which the Lord had given him, and chopped off all the Dragon's six heads, and the rock fell upon the Dragon's body and crushed it to pieces. Then the Prince gathered up the six dragon-heads and laid them on one side, and cut out the six lolling tongues and tied them in his handkerchief, and told the Princess to go back to her palace, for they could not be married for a year and twelve weeks, and if by that time he did not appear, she was to marry another, and with that he departed. Then the coachman of the Princess came up to the place and saw the six heads of the Dragon, and took them up and said to the Princess, "I will slay thee on the spot if thou dost not swear to me twelve times that thou wilt say I slew the Dragon, and wilt take me for thy husband!" Then she swore to it twelve times, for else he would have slain her. So they returned together to the town, and immediately all the black cloth was taken off the houses and the bells fell a-ringing, and all the people rejoiced because the coachman had killed the Dragon. "Let them be married at once!" cried they.

Meanwhile the King's son went on and on till he came to that town where he had left his brother, and there he found that the Tsar and the Tsaritsa had given his brother the whole tsardom and the Tsarivna to wife as well, and there he tarried for a time; but toward the end of a year and twelve weeks he went back to the other city where he had left the Princess, and there he found them making ready for a grand wedding. "What is the meaning of all this?" asked he. And they answered, "The Tsar's coachman has slain the Dragon with six heads and saved the Princess, and now he is to be married to her."--"Good Lord!" cried he, "and I never saw this Dragon! What manner of beast was it?"--Then they took him and showed him the heads of the Dragon, and he cried,

"Good Lord! every other beast hath a tongue, but this Dragon hath none!" Then they told this to the coachman, who had been made a Prince, and the coachman was very angry and said, "Whoever maintains that a Dragon has tongues, him will I order to be tied to four wild horses, and they shall tear him to pieces on the open steppe!" The Princess, however, recognized the King's son, but she held her peace. Then the King's son took out his handkerchief, unrolled it, showed them the six tongues, and put each one into one of the six mouths of the Dragon's six heads, and each of the tongues began to speak and bid the Princess say how the matter went. Then the Princess told how she had knelt down and prayed out of the prayer-book while the King's son slew the Dragon, and how the wicked coachman had made her swear twelve times to that which was false. When the Tsar heard this, he immediately gave the Princess his daughter to the King's son, and they asked him what death the wicked coachman should die. And he answered, "Let him be tied to the tails of four wild horses, and drive them into the endless steppe that they may tear him to pieces there, and the ravens and crows may come and pick his bones."

R. Nisbet Bain

THE UNGRATEFUL CHILDREN AND THE OLD FATHER WHO WENT TO SCHOOL AGAIN

ONCE upon a time there was an old man. He lived to a great age, and God gave him children whom he brought up to man's estate, and he divided all his goods amongst them. "I will pass my remaining days among my children," thought he.

So the old man went to live with his eldest son, and at first the eldest son treated him properly, and did reverence to his old father. "'Tis but meet and right that we should give our father to eat and drink, and see that he has wherewithal to clothe him, and take care to patch up his things from time to time, and let him have clean new shirts on festivals," said the eldest son. So they did so, and at festivals also the old father had his own glass beside him. Thus the eldest son was a good son to his old father. But when the eldest son had been keeping his father for some time he began to regret his hospitality, and was rough to his father, and sometimes even shouted at him. The old man no longer had his own set place in the house as heretofore, and there was none to cut up his food for him. So the eldest son repented him that he had said he would keep his father, and he began to grudge him every morsel of bread that he put in his mouth. The old man had nothing for it but to go to his second son. It might be better for him there or worse, but stay with his eldest son any longer he could not. So the father went to his second son. But here the old man soon discovered that he had only exchanged wheat for straw. Whenever he began to eat, his second son and his daughter-in-law looked sour and murmured something between their teeth. The woman scolded the old man. "We had as much as we could do before to make both ends meet," cried she, "and now we have old men to keep into the bargain." The old man soon had enough of it there also, and went on to his next son. So one after another all four sons took their father to live with them, and he was glad to leave them all. Each of the four sons, one after the other, cast the burden of supporting him on one of the other brothers. "It is for him to keep thee, daddy!" said they; and then the other would say, "Nay, dad, but it is as much as we can do to keep ourselves." Thus between his four sons he knew not what to do. There was quite a battle among them as to which of them should *not* keep their old father. One had one good excuse and another had another, and so none of them would keep him. This one had a lot of little children, and that one had a scold for a wife, and this house was too small, and that house was too poor. "Go where thou wilt, old man," said they, "only don't come to us." And the old man, grey, grey, grey as a dove was he, wept before his sons, and knew not whither to turn. What could he do? Entreaty was in vain. Not one of the sons would take the old man in, and yet he had to be put somewhere. Then the old man strove with them no more, but let them do with him even as they would.

So all four sons met and took counsel. Time after time they laid their heads together, and at last they agreed among themselves that the best thing the old man could do was to go to school. "There will be a bench for him to sit upon there," said they; "and he can take something to eat in his knapsack." Then they told the old man about it; but the old man did not want to go to school. He begged his children not to send him there, and wept before them. "Now that I cannot see the white world," said he, "how can I see a black book? Moreover, from my youth upward I have never learnt my letters; how shall I begin to do so now? A clerk cannot be fashioned out of an old man on the point of death!" But there was no use talking, his children said he *must* go to school, and the voices of his children prevailed against his feeble old voice. So to school he had to go. Now there was no church in that village, so he had to go to the village beyond it to school. A forest lay along the road, and in this forest the old man met a nobleman driving along. When the old man came near to the nobleman's carriage, he stepped out of the road to let it pass, took off his hat respectfully, and then would have gone on farther. But he heard someone calling, and, looking back, saw the nobleman beckoning to him; he wanted to ask him something. The nobleman then got out of his carriage and asked the old man whither he was going. The old man took off his hat to the nobleman and told him all his misery, and the tears ran down the old man's cheeks. "Woe is me, gracious sir! If the Lord had left me without kith and kin, I should not complain; but strange indeed is the woe that has befallen me! I have four sons, thank God, and all four have houses of their own, and yet they send their poor old father to school to learn! Was ever the like of it known before?" So the old man told the nobleman his whole story, and the nobleman was full of compassion for the old man. "Well, old man," said he, "'tis no use for thee to go to school, that's plain. Return home. I'll tell thee what to do so that thy children shall never send thee to school again. Fear not, old man, weep no more, and let not thy soul be troubled! God shall bless thee, and all will be well. I know well what ought to be done here." So the nobleman comforted the old man, and the old man began to be merry. Then the nobleman took out his purse, it was a real nobleman's purse, with a little sack in the middle of it to hold small change. Lord! what a lovely thing it was! The more he looked at it, the more the old man marvelled at it. The nobleman took this purse and began filling it full with something. When he had well filled it, he gave it to the old man. "Take this and go home to thy children," said he, "and when thou hast got home, call together all thy four sons and say to them, 'My dear children, long long ago, when I was younger than I am now, and knocked about in the world a bit, I made a little money. "I won't spend it," I said to myself, "for one never knows what may happen." So I went into a forest, my children, and dug a hole beneath an oak, and there I hid my little store of money. I did not bother much about the money afterward, because I had such good

143

children; but when you sent me to school I came to this self-same oak, and I said to myself, "I wonder if these few silver pieces have been waiting for their master all this time! Let us dig and see." So I dug and found them, and have brought them home to you, my children. I shall keep them till I die; but after my death consult together, and whosoever shall be found to have cherished me most and taken care of me and not grudged me a clean shirt now and then, or a crust of bread when I'm hungry, to him shall be given the greater part of my money. So now, my dear children, receive me back again, and my thanks shall be yours. You can manage it amongst you, and surely 'tis not right that I should seek a home among strangers! Which of you will be kind to your old father––for money?'"

So the old man returned to his children with the purse in a casket, and when he came to the village with the casket under his arm, one could see at once that he had been in a *good forest*.[25] When one comes home with a heavy casket under one's arm, depend upon it there's something in it! So, no sooner did the old man appear than his eldest daughter-in-law came running out to meet him, and bade him welcome in God's name. "Things don't seem to get on at all without thee, dad!" cried she, "and the house is quite dreary. Come in and rest, dad," she went on; "thou hast gone a long way and must be weary." Then all the brothers came together, and the old man told them what God had done for him. All their faces brightened as they looked at the casket, and they thought to themselves, "If we keep him we shall have the money." Then the four brothers could not make too much of their dear old father. They took care of him and the old man was happy, but he took heed to the counsel of the nobleman, and never let the casket out of his hand. "After my death you shall have everything, but I won't give it you now, for who knows what may happen? I have seen already how you treated your old father when he had nothing. It shall all be yours, I say, only wait; and when I die, take it and divide it as I have said." So the brothers tended their father, and the old man lived in clover, and was somebody. He had his own way and did nothing.

So the old man was no longer ill-treated by his children, but lived among them like an emperor in his own empire, but no sooner did he die than his children made what haste they could to lay hands upon the casket. All the people were called together and bore witness that they had treated their father well since he came back to them, so it was adjudged that they should divide the treasure amongst them. But first they took the old man's body to church and the casket along with it. They buried him as God commands. They made a rich banquet of funeral meats that all might know how much they mourned the old man; it was a splendid funeral. When the priest got up from the table, the people all began to thank their hosts, and the eldest son begged the priest to say the *sorokoust*[26] in the church for the repose of the dead man's soul. "Such a dear old fellow as he was!" said he; "was there ever any one like him? Take this money for the *sorokoust*, reverend father!" so horribly grieved was that eldest son. So the eldest son gave the priest money, and the second son gave him the like. Nay, each one gave him money for an extra half *sorokoust*, all four gave him requiem money. "We'll have prayers in church for our father though we sell our last sheep to pay for them," cried they. Then, when all was over, they hastened as fast as they could to the money. The coffer was brought forth. They shook it. There was a fine rattling inside it. Every one of them felt and handled the coffer. That was something like a treasure! Then they unsealed it and opened it and scattered the contents--and it was full of nothing but glass! They wouldn't believe their eyes. They rummaged among the glass, but there was no money. It was horrible! Surely it could not be that their father had dug up a coffer from beneath an oak of the forest and it was full of nothing but glass! "Why!" cried the brothers, "our father has left us nothing but glass!" But for the crowds of people there, the brothers would have fallen upon and beaten each other in their wrath. So the children of the old man saw that their father had made fools of them. Then all the people mocked them: "You see what you have gained by sending your father to school! You see he learned something at school after all! He was a long time before he *began* learning, but better late than never. It appears to us 'twas a right good school you sent him to. No doubt they whipped him into learning so much. Never mind, you can keep the money and the casket!" Then the brothers were full of lamentation and rage. But what could they do? Their father was already dead and buried.

IVAN THE FOOL AND ST PETER'S FIFE

THERE was once upon a time a man who had three sons, and two were clever, but the third, called Ivan, was a fool. Their father divided all his goods among them and died, and the three brothers went out into the world to seek their fortunes. Now the two wise brothers left all their goods at home, but Ivan the fool, who had only inherited a large millstone, took it along with him. They went on and on and on till it began to grow dark, when they came to a large forest. Then the wise brothers said, "Let us climb up to the top of this oak and pass the night there, and then robbers will not fall upon us."--"But what will this silly donkey do with his millstone?" asked one of them.--"You look to yourselves," said Ivan, "for I mean to pass the night in this tree also." Then the wise brothers climbed to the very tip-top of the tree and there sat down, and then Ivan dragged himself up too, and the millstone after him. He tried to get up as high as his brothers, but the thin boughs broke beneath him, so he had to be content with staying in the lower part of the tree on the thicker boughs; so there he sat, hugging the millstone in his arms. Presently some robbers came along that way, red-handed from their work, and they too prepared to pass the night under the tree. So they cut them down firewood, and made them a roaring fire beneath a huge cauldron, and in this cauldron they began to boil their supper. They boiled and boiled till their mess of pottage was ready, and then they all sat down round the cauldron and took out their large ladles, and were just about to fall to--in fact they were blowing their food because it was so boiling hot--when Ivan let his big millstone plump down into the middle of the cauldron, so that the pottage flew right into their eyes. The robbers were so terrified that they all sprang to their feet straightway and

147

scampered off through the forest, forgetting all the booty of which they had robbed the merchantmen. Then Ivan came down from the oak and cried to his brothers, "You come down here and divide the spoil!" So the wise brothers came down, put all the merchandise on the backs of the robbers' horses, and went home with it; but the only thing that Ivan was able to secure for himself was a bag of incense. This he immediately took to the nearest churchyard, placed it on the top of a tomb, and began to pound away at it with his millstone. Suddenly St Peter appeared to him and said, "What art thou doing, good man?"--"I am pounding up this incense to make bread of it."--"Nay, good man, I will advise thee better: give me the incense and take from me whatever thou wilt."--"Very well, St Peter," said the fool; "thou must give me a little fife, but a fife of such a sort that whenever I play upon it, everyone will be obliged to dance."--"But dost thou know how to play upon a fife?"--"No, but I can soon learn." Then St Peter drew forth a little fife from his bosom and gave it to him, and took away the incense, and who can say where he went with it? But Ivan stood up and gazed at the sky and said, "Look now! if St Peter hath not already burnt my incense and made of it that large white cloud that is sailing above my head!" Then he took up his fife and began to play, and the moment he began to play, everything around him began to dance; the wolves, and the hares, and the foxes, and the bears, nay, the very birds lit down upon the ground and began to dance, and Ivan went on laughing and playing all the time. Even the savage, surly bears danced and danced till their legs tottered beneath them. Then they clutched tight hold of the trees to stop themselves from dancing; but it was of no use, dance they must. At last Ivan himself was tired, and lay down to rest, and when he had rested a little, he got up again and went on into the town. There all the people were in the bazaars, buying and selling. Some were buying pancakes, others baskets of bright-coloured eggs, others again pitchers of *kvas*. Ivan began playing on his fife, and forthwith they all fell a-dancing. One man who had a whole basket of eggs on his head danced them into bits, and danced and danced till he looked like the yolk of an egg

148

himself. Those who were asleep got up and gave themselves up to dancing straightway; there were some who danced without trousers, and some who danced without smocks or shirts, and there were some who danced with nothing on at all, for dance they must when Ivan began a-playing. The whole town was turned upside down: the dogs, the swine, the cocks and hens, everything that had life came out and danced. At last Ivan was tired, so he left off playing and went into the town to seek service. The parson there took a fancy to him, and said to him, "Good man! wilt enter my service?"--"That will I, gladly," said Ivan.-- "How much wages dost thou want by the year then?"--"It won't come dear; five *karbovantsya*[27] are all I ask."--"Good, I agree," said the parson. So he engaged Ivan as his servant, and the next day he sent him out into the fields to tend his cattle. Ivan drove the cattle into the pastures, but he himself perched on the top of a haystack while the cattle grazed. He sat there, and sat and sat till he grew quite dull, and then he said to himself, "I'll play a bit on my fife, I haven't played for a long time." So he began to play, and immediately all the cattle fell a-dancing; and not only the cattle, but all the foxes, and the hares, and the wolves, and everything in the hedges and ditches fell a-dancing too. They danced and danced till the poor cattle were clean worn out and at the last gasp. In the evening Ivan drove them home, but they were so famished that they tugged at the dirty straw roofs of the huts they passed, and so got a chance mouthful or two. But Ivan went in and had supper and a comfortable night's rest afterward. The next day he again drove the cattle into the pastures. They began grazing till he took out his fife again, when they all fell a-dancing like mad. He played on and on till evening, when he drove the cattle home again, and they were all as hungry as could be, and wearied to death from dancing.

SUDDENLY ST PETER APPEARED TO HIM

Now the parson was not a little astonished when he saw his cattle. "Where on earth has he been feeding them?" thought he; "they are quite tired out and almost famished! I'll take care to go myself to-morrow, and see exactly whither he takes them, and what he does with them." On the third day the neat-herd again drove the cattle into the pastures, but this time the parson followed after them, and went and hid himself behind the hedge near to which Ivan was watching the cattle graze. There he sat then, and watched to see what the man would do. Presently Ivan mounted on to the haystack and began to play. And immediately all the cattle fell a-dancing, and everything in the hedge, and the parson behind the hedge danced too. Now the hedge was a quickset hedge, and as the parson began capering about in it, he tore to shreds his cassock and his breeches, and his under-coat, and his shirt, and scratched his skin and wrenched out his beard as if he had been very badly shaved, and still the poor parson had to go on dancing in the midst of the prickly hedge till there were great weals and wounds all over his body, and the red blood began to flow. Then the parson saw he was in evil case, and shrieked to his herdsman to leave off playing; but the herdsman was so wrapped up in his music that he did not hear him; but at last he looked in the direction of the hedge, and when he saw the poor parson skipping about like a lunatic, he stopped. The parson darted away as fast as his legs could carry him toward the village, and oh! what a sight he looked as he dashed through the streets! The people didn't know him, and--scandalized that anybody should run about in rags and tatters so that his whole body could be seen--began to hoot him. Then the poor man turned aside from the public road, crawled off through the woods, and dashed off through the tall reeds of the gardens, with the dogs after him. For wherever he went they took him for a robber, and hounded on the dogs. At last the parson got home, all rags and tatters, so that when his wife saw him she did not know him, but called to the labourers, "Help, help! here's a robber, turn him out!" They came rushing up with sticks and cudgels, but he began talking to them, and at last they recognized him, led him home, and he told his wife all about Ivan. The parson's wife was so amazed she could scarce believe it. In the evening Ivan drove home the oxen, put them into their stalls, gave them straw to eat, and then came into the house himself to have supper. He came into the house, and the parson said to him, "Come now, Ivan, when thou hast rested a bit, play my wife a little song!" But as for the parson, he took good care to tie himself first of all to the pillar which held up the roof of the house. Ivan sat down on the ground near to the threshold and began to play. The parson's wife sat down on the bench to listen to him while he played; but immediately she leaped up from the bench and began to dance, and she danced with such hearty good-will that the place became too small for her. Then the Devil seemed to take possession of the cat too, for pussy leaped from under the stove and began to spring and bound about also. The parson held on and held on to the pillar with all his might, but it was of no use. He had no power to resist; he let go with his hands, and tugged and tugged till the rope that held him grew slacker and slacker, and then he went dancing round and round the pillar at a furious rate, with the rope chafing his hands and feet all the time. At last he could endure it no longer, and bawled to Ivan to stop. "The deuce is in thee!" cried he. Then Ivan stopped playing, put his fife into his breast-pocket, and went and lay down to sleep. But the parson said to his wife, "We must turn away this Ivan to-morrow, for he will be the death of ourselves and our cattle!" Ivan, however, overheard what the parson said to his wife, and getting up early in the morning, he went straight to the parson, and said to him, "Give me one hundred *karbovantsya*, and I'll be off; but if you won't give them to me, I'll play and play till you and your wife have danced yourselves to death, and then I'll take your place and live at mine ease." The parson scratched himself behind the ears and hesitated; but at last he thought he had better give the money and be quit of him. So he took the hundred *karbovantsya* out of his satchel and gave them to Ivan. Then Ivan played them a parting song, till the parson and his wife fell down to the ground, dead-beat, with their tongues lolling out of their mouths; and then he put his fife into his breast-pocket, and wandered forth into the wide world.

R. Nisbet Bain

THE MAGIC EGG

THERE was once upon a time a lark who was the Tsar among the birds, and he took unto himself as his Tsaritsa a little shrew-mouse. They had a field all to themselves, which they sowed with wheat, and when the wheat grew up they divided it between them, when they found that there was one grain over! The mouse said, "Let me have it!" But the lark said, "No, let me have it!"-- "What's to be done?" thought they. They would have liked to take counsel of some one, but they had no parents or kinsmen, nobody at all to whom they could go and ask advice in the matter. At last the mouse said, "At any rate, let me have the first nibble!" The lark Tsar agreed to this; but the little mouse fastened her teeth in it and ran off into her hole with it, and there ate it all up. At this the Tsar lark was wrath, and collected all the birds of the air to make war upon the mouse Tsaritsa; but the Tsaritsa called together all the beasts to defend her, and so the war began. Whenever the beasts came rushing out of the wood to tear the birds to pieces, the birds flew up into the trees; but the birds kept in the air, and hacked and pecked the beasts wherever they could. Thus they fought the whole day, and in the evening they lay down to rest. Now when the Tsaritsa looked around upon her forces, she saw that the ant was taking no part in the war. She immediately went and commanded the ant to be there by evening, and when the ant came, the Tsaritsa ordered her to climb up the trees with her kinsmen and bite off the feathers round the birds' wings.

Next day, when there was light enough to see by, the mouse Tsaritsa cried, "Up, up, my warriors!" Thereupon the birds also rose up, and immediately fell to the ground, where the beasts tore them to bits. So the Tsaritsa overcame the Tsar. But there was one eagle who saw there was something wrong, so he did not try to fly, but remained sitting on the tree. And lo! there came an archer along that way, and seeing the eagle on the tree, he took aim at it; but the eagle besought him and said, "Do not kill me, and I'll be of great service to thee!" The archer aimed a second time, but the eagle besought him still more and said, "Take me down rather and keep me, and thou shalt see that it will be to thy advantage." The archer, however, took aim a third time, but the eagle began to beg of him most piteously, "Nay, kill me not, but take me home with thee, and thou shalt see what great advantage it will be to thee!" The archer believed the bird. He climbed up the tree, took the eagle down, and carried it home. Then the eagle said to him, "Put me in a hut, and feed me with flesh till my wings have grown again."

Now this archer had two cows and a steer, and he at once killed and cut up one of the cows for the eagle. The eagle fed upon this cow for a full year, and then he said to the archer, "Let me go, that I may fly. I see that my wings have already grown again!" Then the archer let him loose from the hut. The eagle flew round and round, he flew about for half a day, and then he returned to the archer and said, "I feel I have but little strength in me, slay me another cow!" And the archer obeyed him, and slew the second cow, and the eagle lived upon that for yet another year. Again the eagle flew round and round in the air. He flew round and about the whole day till evening, when he returned to the archer and said, "I am stronger than I was, but I have still but little strength in me, slay me the steer also!" Then the man thought to himself, "What shall I do? Shall I slay it, or shall I not slay it?" At last he said, "Well! I've sacrificed more than this before, so let this go too!" and he took the steer and slaughtered it for the eagle. Then the eagle lived upon this for another whole year longer, and after that he took to flight, and flew high up right to the very clouds. Then he flew down again to the man and said to him, "I thank thee, brother, for that thou hast been the saving of me! Come now and sit upon me!"--"Nay, but," said the man, "what if some evil befall me?"--"Sit on me, I say!" cried the eagle. So the archer sat down upon the bird.

Then the eagle bore him nearly as high as the big clouds, and then let him fall. Down plumped the man; but the eagle did not let him fall to the earth, but swiftly flew beneath him and upheld him, and said to him, "How dost thou feel now?"--"I feel," said the man, "as if I had no life in me."--Then the eagle replied, "That was just how I felt when thou didst aim at me the first time." Then he said to him, "Sit on my back again!" The man did not want to sit on him, but what could he do? Sit he must. Then the eagle flew with him quite as high as the big clouds, and shook him off, and down he fell headlong till he was about two fathoms from the ground, when the bird again flew beneath him and held him up. Again the eagle asked him, "How dost thou feel?" And the man replied, "I feel just as if all my bones were already broken to bits!"--"That is just how I felt when thou didst take aim at me the second time," replied the eagle. "But now sit on my back once more." The man did so, and the eagle flew with him as high as the small fleecy clouds, and then he shook him off, and down he fell headlong; but when he was but a hand's-breadth from the earth, the eagle again flew beneath him and held him up, and said to him, "How dost thou feel now?" And he replied, "I feel as if I no longer belonged to this world!"--"That is just how I felt when thou didst aim at me the third time," replied the eagle. "But now," continued the bird, "thou art guilty no more. We are quits. I owe thee naught, and thou owest naught to me; so sit on my back again, and I'll take thee to my master."

They flew on and on, they flew till they came to the eagle's uncle. And the eagle said to the archer, "Go to my house, and when they ask thee, 'Hast thou not seen our poor child?' reply, 'Give me the magic egg, and I'll bring him before your eyes!'" So he went to the house, and there they said to him, "Hast thou heard of our poor child with thine ears, or seen him with thine eyes, and hast thou come hither willingly or unwillingly?"--And he answered, "I have come hither willingly!"--Then they asked, "Hast thou smelt out anything of our poor youngster? for it is three years now since he went to the wars, and there's neither sight nor sound of him more!"--And he answered, "Give me the magic egg, and I'll bring him straightway before your eyes!"--Then they replied, "'Twere better we never saw him than that we should give thee the magic egg!"--Then he went back to the eagle and said to him, "They said, ''Twere better we never saw him than that we should give thee the magic egg.'"--Then the eagle answered, "Let us fly on farther!"

They flew on and on till they came to the eagle's brother, and the archer said just the same to him as he had said to the eagle's uncle, and still he didn't get the egg. Then they flew to the eagle's father, and the eagle said to him, "Go up to the hut, and if they ask for me, say that thou hast seen me and will bring me before their eyes."--So he went up to the hut, and they said to him, "O Tsarevich, we hear thee with our ears and see thee with our eyes, but hast thou come hither of thine own free will or by the will of another?"--And the archer answered, "I have come hither of my own free will!"--Then they asked him, "Hast thou seen our son? Lo, these four years we have not had news of him. He went off to the wars, and perchance he has been slain there."--And he answered them, "I have seen him, and if you will give me the magic egg, I will bring him before your eyes."--And the eagle's father said to him, "What good will such a thing do thee? We had better give thee the lucky penny!"--But he answered, "I don't want the lucky penny, give me the magic egg!"--"Come hither then," said he, "and thou shalt have it." So he went into the hut. Then the eagle's father rejoiced and gave him the egg, and said to him, "Take heed thou dost not break it anywhere on the road, and when thou gettest home, hedge it round and build a strong fence about it, and it will do thee good."

So he went homeward. He went on and on till a great thirst came upon him. So he stopped at the first spring he came to, and as he stooped to drink he stumbled and the magic egg was broken. Then he perceived that an ox had come out of the egg and was rolling away. He gave chase to the ox, but whenever he was getting close to one side of it, the other side of it got farther away from him. Then the poor fellow cried, "I shall do nothing with it myself, I see."--At that moment an old she-dragon came up to him and said, "What wilt thou give me, O man, if I chase this ox back again into the egg for thee?"--And the archer replied, "What *can* I give?"--The dragon said to him, "Give me what thou hast at home without thy will and wit!"--"Done!" said the archer. Then the dragon chased the ox nicely into the egg again, patched it up prettily and gave it into the man's hand. Then the archer went home, and when he got home he found a son had been born to him there, and his son said to him, "Why didst thou give me to the old she-dragon, dad? But never mind, I'll manage to live in spite of her." Then the father was very grieved for a time, but what could he do? Now the name of this son was Ivan.

So Ivan lost no time in going to the dragon, and the dragon said to him, "Go to my house and do me three tasks, and if thou dost them not, I'll devour thee." Now, round the dragon's house was a large meadow as far as the eye could reach. And the dragon said to him, "Thou must in a single night weed out this field and sow wheat in it, and reap the wheat and store it, all in this very night; and thou must bake me a roll out of this self-same wheat, and the roll must be lying ready for me on my table in the morning."

Then Ivan went and leaned over the fence, and his heart within him was sore troubled. Now near to him there was a post, and on this post was the dragon's starveling daughter. So when he came thither and fell a-weeping, she asked him, "Wherefore dost thou weep?"--And he said, "How can I help weeping? The dragon has bidden me do something I can never, never do; and what is more, she has bidden me do it in a single night."--"What is it, pray?" asked the dragon's daughter. Then he told her. "Not every bush bears a berry!" cried she. "Promise to take me to wife, and I'll do all she has bidden thee do." He promised, and then she said to him again, "Now go and lie down, but see that thou art up early in the morning to bring her her roll." Then she went to the field, and before one could whistle she had cleaned it of weeds and harrowed it and sown it with wheat, and by dawn she had reaped the wheat and cooked the roll and brought it to him, and said, "Now, take it to her hut and put it on her table."

Then the old she-dragon awoke and came to the door, and was amazed at the sight of the field, which was now all stubble, for the corn had been cut. Then she said to Ivan, "Yes, thou hast done the work well. But now, see that thou doest my second task." Then she gave him her second command. "Dig up that mountain yonder and let the Dnieper flow over the site of it, and there build a store-house, and in the store-house stack the wheat that thou hast reaped, and sell this wheat to the merchant barques that sail by, and everything must be done by the time I get up early next morning!" Then he again went to the fence and wept, and the maiden said to him, "Why dost thou weep?" and he told her all that the she-dragon had bidden him do. "There are lots of bushes, but where are the berries? Go and lie down, and I'll do it all for thee." Then she whistled, and the mountain was levelled and the Dnieper flowed over the site of it, and round about the Dnieper store-houses rose up, and then she came and woke him that he might go and sell the wheat to the merchant barques that sailed by that way, and when the she-dragon rose up early in the morning she was amazed to see that everything had been done which she had commanded him.

Then she gave him her third command. "This night thou must catch the golden hare, and bring it to me by the morning light." Again he went to the fence and fell a-weeping. And the girl asked him, "Why art thou weeping?"--He said to her, "She has ordered me to catch her the golden hare."--"Oh, oh!" cried the she-dragon's daughter, "the berries are ripening now; only her father knows how to catch such a hare as that. Nevertheless, I'll go to a rocky place I know of, and there perchance we shall be able to catch it." So they went to this rocky place together, and she said to him, "Stand over that hole. I'll go in and chase him out of the hole, and do thou catch him as he comes out; but mind, whatever comes out of the hole, seize it, for it will be the golden hare."

So she went and began beating up, and all at once out came a snake and hissed, and he let it go. Then she came out of the hole and said to him, "What! has nothing come out?"--"Well," said he, "only a snake, and I was afraid it would bite me, so I let it go."-- "What hast thou done?" said she; "that was the very hare itself. Look now!" said she, "I'll go in again, and if any one comes out and tells you that the golden hare is not here, don't believe it, but hold him fast." So she crept into the hole again and began to beat for game, and out came an old woman, who said to the youth, "What art thou poking about there for?"--And he said to her, "For the golden hare."--She said to him, "It is not here, for this is a snake's hole," and when she had said this she went away. Presently the girl also came out and said to him, "What! hast thou not got the hare? Did nothing come out then?"--"No," said he, "nothing but an old woman who asked me what I was seeking, and I told her the golden hare, and she said, 'It is not here,' so I let her go."--Then the girl replied, "Why didst thou not lay hold of her? for she was the very golden hare itself, and now thou never wilt catch it unless I turn myself into a hare and thou take and lay me on the table, and give me into my mother's, the she-dragon's hands, and go away, for if she find out all about it she will tear the pair of us to pieces."

So she changed herself into a hare, and he took and laid her on the table, and said to the she-dragon, "There's thy hare for thee, and now let me go away!" She said to him, "Very well--be off!" Then he set off running, and he ran and ran as hard as he could. Soon after, the old she-dragon discovered that it was not the golden hare, but her own daughter, so she set about chasing after them to destroy them both, for the daughter had made haste in the meantime to join Ivan. But as the she-dragon couldn't run herself, she sent her husband, and he began chasing them, and they knew he was coming, for they felt the earth trembling beneath his tread. Then the she-dragon's daughter said to Ivan, "I hear him running after us. I'll turn myself into standing wheat and thee into an old man guarding me, and if he ask thee, 'Hast thou seen a lad and a lass pass by this way?' say to him, 'Yes, they passed by this way while I was sowing this wheat!'"

A little while afterward the she-dragon's husband came flying up. "Have a lad and a lass passed by this way?" said he. "Yes," replied the old man, "they have."--"Was it long ago?" asked the she-dragon's husband.--"It was while this wheat was being sown," replied the old man.--"Oh!" thought the dragon, "this wheat is ready for the sickle, they couldn't have been this way yesterday," so he turned back. Then the she-dragon's daughter turned herself back into a maiden and the old man into a youth, and off they set again. But the dragon returned home, and the she-dragon asked him, "What! hast thou not caught them or met them on the road?"--"Met them, no!" said he. "I did, indeed, pass on the road some standing wheat and an old man watching it, and I asked the old man if he had seen a lad and a lass pass by that way, and he said, 'Yes, while this wheat was being sown,' but the wheat was quite ripe for the sickle, so I knew it was a long while ago and turned back."--"Why didst thou not tear that old man and the wheat to pieces?" cried the she-dragon; "it was they! Be off after them again, and mind, this time tear them to pieces without fail."

So the dragon set off after them again, and they heard him coming from afar, for the earth trembled beneath him, so the damsel said to Ivan, "He's coming again, I hear him; now I'll change myself into a monastery, so old that it will be almost falling to pieces, and I'll change thee into an old black monk at the gate, and when he comes up and asks, 'Hast thou seen a lad and a lass pass this way?' say to him, 'Yes, they passed by this way when this monastery was being built.'" Soon afterward the dragon came flying past, and asked the monk, "Hast thou seen a lad and a lass pass by this way?"--"Yes," he replied, "I saw them what time the holy fathers began to build this monastery." The dragon thought to himself, "That was not yesterday! This monastery has stood a hundred years if it has stood a day, and won't stand much longer either," and with that he turned him back. When he got home, he said to the she-dragon, his wife, "I met a black monk who serves in a monastery, and I asked him about them, and he told me that a lad and a lass had run past that way when the monastery was being built, but that was not yesterday, for the monastery is a hundred years old at the very least."--"Why didst thou not tear the black monk to pieces and pull down the monastery? for 'twas they. But I see I must go after them myself, thou art no good at all."

So off she set and ran and ran, and they knew she was coming, for the earth quaked and yawned beneath her. Then the damsel said to Ivan, "I fear me 'tis all over, for she is coming herself! Look now! I'll change thee into a stream and myself into a fish--a perch." Immediately after the she-dragon came up and said to the perch, "Oh, oh! so thou wouldst run away from me, eh!" Then she turned herself into a pike and began chasing the perch, but every time she drew near to it, the perch turned its prickly fins toward her, so that she could not catch hold of it. So she kept on chasing it and chasing it, but finding she could not catch it, she tried to drink up the stream, till she drank so much of it that she burst.

Then the maiden who had become a fish said to the youth who had become a river, "Now that we are alive and not dead, go back to thy lord-father and thy father's house and see them, and kiss them all except the daughter of thy uncle, for if thou kiss that damsel thou wilt forget me, and I shall go to the land of Nowhere." So he went home and greeted them all, and as he did so he thought to himself, "Why should I not greet my uncle's daughter like the rest of them? Why, they'll think me a mere pagan if I don't!" So he kissed her, and the moment he did so he forgot all about the girl who had saved him.

So he remained there half a year, and then bethought him of taking to himself a wife. So they betrothed him to a very pretty girl, and he accepted her and forgot all about the other girl who had saved him from the dragon, though she herself was the she-dragon's daughter. Now the evening before the wedding they heard a young damsel crying *Shishki*[28] in the streets. They called to the young damsel to go away, or say who she was, for nobody knew her. But the damsel answered never a word, but began to knead more cakes, and made a cock-dove and a hen-dove out of the dough and put them down on the ground, and they became alive. And the hen-dove said to the cock-dove, "Hast thou forgotten how I cleared the field for thee, and sowed it with wheat, and thou mad'st a roll from the corn which thou gavest to the she-dragon?"--But the cock-dove answered, "Forgotten! forgotten!"--Then she said to him again, "And hast thou forgotten how I dug away the mountain for thee, and let the Dnieper flow by it that the merchant barques might come to thy store-houses, and that thou mightst sell thy wheat to the merchant barques?" But the cock-dove replied, "Forgotten! forgotten!"-- Then the hen-dove said to him again, "And hast thou forgotten how we two went together in search of the golden hare? Hast thou forgotten me then altogether?"--And the cock-dove answered again, "Forgotten! forgotten!" Then the good youth Ivan bethought him who this damsel was that had made the doves, and he took her to his arms and made her his wife, and they lived happily ever afterward.

THE STORY OF THE FORTY-FIRST BROTHER

THERE was once upon a time an old man who had forty-one sons. Now when this old man was at the point of death, he divided all he had among his sons, and gave to each of the forty a horse; but when he came to the forty-first he found he had no more horses left, so the forty-first brother had to be content with a foal. When their father was dead, the brothers said to each other, "Let us go to Friday and get married!"--But the eldest brother said, "No, Friday has only forty daughters, so one of us would be left without a bride."--Then the second brother said, "Let us go then to Wednesday--Wednesday has forty-one daughters, and so the whole lot of us can pair off with the whole lot of them." So they went and chose their brides. The eldest brother took the eldest sister, and the youngest the youngest, till they were all suited. And the youngest brother of all said, "I'll take that little damsel who is sitting on the stove in the corner and has the nice kerchief in her hand." Then they all drank a bumper together to seal the bargain, and after that the forty-one bridegrooms and the forty-one brides laid them down to sleep side by side. But the youngest brother of all said to himself, "I will bring my foal into the room." So he brought in the foal, and then went to his bedchamber and laid him down to sleep also. Now his bride lay down with her kerchief in her hand, and he took a great fancy to it, and he begged and prayed her for it again and again, until at last she gave it to him. Now, when Wednesday thought that all the people were asleep, he went out into the courtyard to sharpen his sabre. Then the foal said, "Oh, my dear little master, come here, come here!" He came, and the foal said to him, "Take off the night-dresses of the forty sleeping bridegrooms and put them on the forty sleeping brides, and put the night-dresses of the brides
165

on the bridegrooms, for a great woe is nigh!" And he did so. When Wednesday had sharpened his sabre he came into the room and began feeling for the stiff collars of the bridegrooms' night-dresses, and straightway cut off the forty heads above the collars. Then he carried off the heads of his forty daughters in a bunch (for the brides now had on the night-dresses of their bridegrooms), and went and lay down to sleep. Then the foal said, "My dear little father! awake the bridegrooms, and we'll set off." So he awoke the bridegrooms and sent them on before, while he followed after on his own little nag. They trotted on and on, and at last the foal said to him, "Look behind, and see whether Wednesday is not pursuing." He looked round: "Yes, little brother," said he, "Wednesday *is* pursuing!"--"Shake thy kerchief then!" said the foal. He shook his kerchief, and immediately a vast sea was between him and the pursuer. Then they went on and on till the foal said to him again, "Look behind, and see if Wednesday is still pursuing!"--He looked round. "Yes, little brother, he *is* pursuing!"--"Wave thy handkerchief on the left side!" said the foal. He waved it on the left side, and immediately between them and the pursuer stood a forest so thick that not even a little mouse could have squeezed through it. Then they went on still farther, till the foal said again, "Look behind, and see whether Wednesday is still pursuing!"--He looked behind, and there, sure enough, was Wednesday running after them, and he was not very far off either.--"Wave thy kerchief!" said the foal. He waved his kerchief, and immediately a steep mountain--oh, so steep!--lay betwixt them. They went on and on, until the foal said again, "Look behind, is Wednesday still pursuing?"--So he looked behind him and said, "No, now he is not there." Then they went on and on again, and soon they were not very far from home. Then the youngest brother said, "You go home now, but I am going to seek a bride!" So he went on and on till he came to a place where lay a feather of the bird Zhar. "Look!" cried he, "what I've found!"--But the foal said to him, "Pick not up that feather, for it will bring thee evil as well as good!"--But his master said, "Why, I should be a fool not to pick up a feather like that!" So he turned back and picked up the feather. Then he went on farther and farther, until he came to a clay hut. He went into this clay hut, and there sat an old woman. "Give me a night's lodging, granny!" said he.--"I have neither bed nor light to offer thee," said she. Nevertheless he entered the hut and put the feather on the window-corner, and it lit up the whole hut. So he went to sleep. But the old woman ran off to the Tsar, and said to him, "A certain man has come to me and laid a certain feather on the window-sill, and it shines like fire!" Then the Tsar guessed that it was a feather of the bird Zhar, and said to his soldiers, "Go and fetch that man hither!" And the Tsar said to him, "Wilt thou enter my service?"-- "Yes," he replied, "but you must give me all your keys." So the Tsar gave him all the keys and a hut of his own to live in besides. But one day the Tsar said to his servants, "Boil me now a vat of milk!" So they boiled it. Then he took off his gold ring, and said to the man, "Thou didst get the feather of the bird Zhar, get me also this golden ring of mine out of the vat of boiling milk!"--"Bring hither, then, my faithful horse," said he, "that he may see his master plunge into the vat of boiling milk and die!" So they brought his horse, and, taking off his clothes, he plunged into the vat, but as he did so the horse snorted so violently that all the boiling milk leaped up in the air and the man seized the ring and gave it back to the Tsar. Now when the Tsar saw that the man had come out of the vat younger and handsomer than ever, he said, "I'll try and fish up the ring in like manner." So he flung his ring into the vat of boiling milk and plunged after it to get it. The people waited and waited and wondered and wondered that he was so long about it, and at last they drained off the milk and found the Tsar at the bottom of the vat boiled quite red. Then the man said, "Now, Tsaritsa, thou art mine and I am thine." And they lived together happily ever afterward.

R. NISBET BAIN

THE STORY OF THE UNLUCKY DAYS

AT the end of a village on the verge of the steppe dwelt two brothers, one rich and the other poor. One day the poor brother came to the rich brother's house and sat down at his table; but the rich brother drove him away and said, "How durst thou sit at my table? Be off! Thy proper place is in the fields to scare away the crows!" So the poor brother went into the fields to scare away the crows. The crows all flew away when they saw him, but among them was a raven that flew back again and said to him, "O man! in this village thou wilt never be able to live, for here there is neither luck nor happiness for thee, but go into another village and thou shalt do well!" Then the man went home, called together his wife and children, put up the few old clothes that still remained in his wardrobe, and went on to the next village, carrying his water-skin on his shoulders. On and on they tramped along the road, but the Unlucky Days clung on to the man behind, and said, "Why dost thou not take us with thee? We will never leave thee, for thou art ours!" So they went on with him till they came to a river, and the man, who was thirsty, went down to the water's edge for a drink. He undid his water-skin, persuaded the Unlucky Days to get into it, tied it fast again and buried it on the bank close by the river. Then he and his family went on farther. They went on and on till they came to another village, and at the very end of it was an empty hut--the people who had lived there had died of hunger. There the whole family settled down. One day they were all sitting down there when they heard something in the mountain crying, "Catch hold! catch hold! catch hold!" The man went at once into his stable, took down the bit and reins that remained to him, and climbed up into the mountain. He looked all about him as he went, and at last he saw, sitting down, an old

169

goat with two large horns––it was the Devil himself, but of course he didn't know that. So he made a lasso of the reins, threw them round the old goat, and began to drag it gently down the mountain-side. He dragged it all the way up the ladder of his barn, when the goat disappeared, but showers and showers of money came tumbling through the ceiling. He collected them all together, and they filled two large coffers. Then the poor man made the most of his money, and in no very long time he was well-to-do. Then he sent some of his people to his rich brother, and invited him to come and live with him. The rich brother pondered the matter over. "Maybe he has nothing to eat," thought he, "and that is why he sends for me." So he bade them bake him a good store of fat pancakes, and set out accordingly. On the way he heard that his brother had grown rich, and the farther he went the more he heard of his brother's wealth. Then he regretted that he had brought all the pancakes with him, so he threw them away into the ditch. At last he came to his brother's house, and his brother showed him first one of the coffers full of money and then the other. Then envy seized upon the rich brother, and he grew quite green in the face. But his brother said to him, "Look now! I have buried a lot more money in a water-skin, hard by the river; you may dig it up and keep it if you like, for I have lots of my own here!" The rich brother did not wait to be told twice. Off he went to the river, and began digging up the water-skin straightway. He unfastened it with greedy, trembling hands; but he had no sooner opened it than the Unlucky Days all popped out and clung on to him. "Thou art ours!" said they. He went home, and when he got there he found that all his wealth was consumed, and a heap of ashes stood where his house had been. So he went and lived in the place where his brother had lived, and the Unlucky Days lived with him ever afterward.

THE WONDROUS STORY OF IVAN GOLIK AND THE SERPENTS

SOMEWHERE, nowhere, in another kingdom, in the Empire of Thrice-ten, lived––whether 'twas a Tsar and a Tsaritsa, or only a Prince and a Princess, I know not, but anyhow they had two sons. One day this prince said to his sons, "Let us go down to the seashore and listen to the songs of the sea-folk!" So they went. Now the prince wanted to test the wits of his two sons; he wanted to see which of the twain was fit for ruling his empire, and which should stand aside and make way for better men. So they went on together till they came to where three oaks stood all in a row. The prince looked at the trees, and said to his eldest son, "My dear son, what wouldst thou make of those trees?"

"What would I make of them, dear father? I would make me good barns and store-houses out of them. I would cut them down and plane the timber well, and goodly should be the planks I should make of them."

"Good, my son!" replied the prince, "thou wilt make a careful householder."

Then he asked his younger son, "And what wouldst thou make out of these oaks, my son?"

"Well, dear father," said he, "had I only as much power as will, I would cut down the middle oak, lay it across the other two, and hang up every prince and every noble in the wide world."

Then the prince shook his head and was silent.

Presently they came to the sea, and all three stood still and looked at it, and watched the fishes play. Then, suddenly, the prince

171

caught hold of his younger son, and pitched him right into the sea. "Perish!" cried he, "for 'tis but just that such a wretch as thou shouldst perish!"

Now, just as the father pitched his younger son into the sea, a great whale-fish was coming along and swallowed him, and into its maw he went. There he found wagons with horses and oxen harnessed to them, all of which the fish had also gobbled. So he went rummaging about these wagons to see what was in them, and he found that one of the wagons was full of tobacco-pipes and tobacco, and flints and steels. So he took up a pipe, filled it with tobacco, lit it, and began to smoke. He smoked out one pipe, filled another, and smoked that too; then he filled a third, and began smoking that. At last the smoke inside the whale made it feel so uncomfortable that it opened its mouth, swam ashore, and went asleep on the beach. Now some huntsmen happened to be going along the beach at that time, and one of them saw the whale, and said, "Look, my brethren! we have been hunting jays and crows and shot nothing, and lo! what a monstrous fish lies all about the shore! Let us shoot it!"

So they shot at it and shot at it, and then they fell upon it with their axes and began to cut it to pieces. They cut and hacked at it till suddenly they heard something calling to them from the middle of the fish, "Ho! my brothers! hack fish if you like, but hack not that flesh which is full of Christian blood!"

They fell down to the ground for fright, and were like dead men, but the prince's younger son crept out of the hole in the fish that the huntsmen had made, went out upon the shore, and sat down. He sat down there quite naked, for all his clothes had rotted and dropped off inside the fish. Maybe he had been a whole year in the whale without knowing it, and he thought to himself, "How shall I now manage to live in the wide, wide world?"

Meanwhile the elder brother had become a great nobleman. His father had died, and he was lord over his whole inheritance. Then, as is the wont of princes, he called together his senators and his servants, and they counselled their young prince to marry; so out he went to seek a bride, and a great retinue followed after him. They went on and on till they came to where a naked man was sitting. Then the prince said to one of his servants, "Go and see what manner of man that is!"

So the servant went up to the man, and said, "Hail!"

"Hail to thee!"

"Who art thou, prythee?"

"I am Ivan Golik.[29] Who art thou?"

"We are from such and such a land, and we are going with our prince to seek him a bride."

"Go, tell thy prince that he must take me with him, for he'll make no good match without me."

So the messenger returned to the prince and told him. Then the prince bade his servants open his trunk and take out a shirt and pantaloons and all manner of raiment, whereupon the naked man went into the water and washed, and after that he dressed himself. Then they brought him to the prince, and he said to him, "If you take me with you, you must all obey me. If you listen to me, you shall remain in the land of Russia; but if not, you shall all perish."

"Be it so!" said the prince, and he bade all his suite obey him.

They went on and on till they overtook the hosts of the mice. The prince wanted to go hunting after the mice, but Ivan Golik said, "Nay, step aside and give place to the mice, so that not a single one of them lose a single hair!"

So they turned aside, and the mice swept by in their hosts, but the hindmost mouse turned round and said, "Thanks to thee, Ivan Golik, thou hast saved my host from perishing; I will save thine also."

R. NISBET BAIN

Then they went on farther, and lo! the gnat was marching with his host, and so vast was it that no eye could take it all in. Then the lieutenant-general of the gnats came flying up and said, "Oh, Ivan Golik! let my host drink of thy blood. If thou dost consent, 'twill be to thy profit; but if thou dost not consent, thou shalt not remain in the land of Russia."

Then he stripped off his shirt and bade them tie him up so that he could not beat off a single gnat, and the gnats drank their fill of him and flew off again.

After that they went along by the seashore till they came to a man who had caught two pike. Then Ivan Golik said to the prince, "Buy those two pike of the man, and let them go into the sea again."

"But wherefore?"

"Ask not wherefore, but buy them!"

So they bought the pike, and let them go into the sea again. But as they swam away, the pike turned round and said, "We thank thee, Ivan Golik, that thou hast not let us perish, and it shall be to thy weal and welfare!"

Swiftly they moved on their way, but the story that tells thereof moves still swifter. They went on and on, for more than a month maybe, till they came to another land and to another tsardom, to the Empire of Thrice-ten. And the serpent was the Tsar of that tsardom. Vast were his palaces, iron railings surrounded his courtyards, and the railings were covered with the heads of various warriors; only on the twenty huge pillars in front of the gate were there no heads. As they drew nigh, deadly fear oppressed the heart of the prince, and he said to Ivan, "Mark me, Ivan! those pillars yonder are meant for *our* heads!"--"That remains to be seen," replied Ivan Golik.

When they arrived there, the serpent at first treated them hospitably as welcome guests. They were all to come in and make merry, he said, but the prince he took to his own house. So they

174

ate and drank together, and the thoughts of their hearts were joyous. Now the serpent had twenty-one daughters, and he brought them to the prince, and told him which was the eldest, and which the next eldest, down to the very last one. But it was the youngest daughter of all that the prince's fancy fed upon more than on any of the others. Thus they diverted themselves till evening, and in the evening they made ready to go to sleep. But the serpent said to the prince, "Well, which of my daughters dost thou think the loveliest?"

"The youngest is the most beautiful," said the prince, "and her will I wed."

"Good!" said the serpent, "but I will not let thee have my daughter till thou hast done all my tasks. If thou doest my tasks, thou shalt have my daughter; but if thou doest them not, thou shalt lose thy head, and all thy suite shall perish with thee."

Then he gave him his first task: "In my barn are three hundred ricks of corn; by the morning light thou shalt have threshed and sifted them so that stalk lies by stalk, chaff by chaff, and grain by grain."

Then the prince went to his own place to pass the night there, and bitterly he wept. But Ivan Golik saw that he was weeping, and said to him, "Why dost thou weep, O prince?"

"Why should I not weep, seeing the task that the serpent has given me is impossible?"

"Nay, weep not, my prince, but lie down to sleep, and by the morning light it will all be done!"

No sooner had Ivan Golik left the prince than he went outside and whistled for the mice. Then the mice assembled round them in their hosts: "Why dost thou whistle, and what dost thou want of us, O Ivan Golik?" said they.

"Why should I not whistle, seeing that the serpent has bidden us thresh out his barn by the morning light, so that straw lies by straw, chaff by chaff, and grain by grain?"

No sooner did the mice hear this than they began scampering all about the barn! There were so many of them that there was not room to move. They set to work with a will, and long before dawn it was quite finished. Then they went and awoke Ivan Golik. He went and looked, and lo! all the chaff was by itself, and all the grain was by itself, and all the straw by itself! Then Ivan bade them be quite sure that there was not a single grain remaining in a single ear of corn. So they scampered all about, and there was not a mouse which did not look under every stalk of straw. Then they ran up to him, and said, "Fear not! there is not a single loose grain anywhere. And now we have requited thee thy service, Ivan Golik, farewell!"

Next morning the prince came to seek Ivan, and marvelled to find that everything had been done as the serpent had commanded. So he thanked Ivan Golik, and went off to the serpent. Then they both went together, and the serpent himself was amazed. He called to his twenty-one daughters to search the ears of corn well to see whether one single grain might not be found therein, and his daughters searched and searched, but there was not a single loose grain to be found. Then said the serpent, "'Tis well, let us go! We will eat and drink and make merry till evening, and in the evening I will give thee thy to-morrow's task." So they made merry till evening, and then the serpent said, "Early this morning, my youngest daughter went bathing in the sea and lost her ring in the water. She searched and searched for it, but could find it nowhere. If thou canst find it to-morrow, and bring it hither while we are sitting down to meat, thou shalt remain alive; if not, 'tis all over with thee!"

The prince returned to his own people and fell a-weeping. Ivan Golik perceived it, and said to him, "Wherefore dost thou weep?"

"For such and such a reason," said he; "dost thou not see that I am ruined?"

Then said Ivan Golik, "The serpent lies. He himself it was who took his daughter's ring and flew over the sea early this morning, and dropped it in the water. But lie down and sleep! I myself will go to the sea to-morrow, haply I may find the ring."

So, very early next morning, Ivan Golik went down to the sea. He shouted with an heroic voice, and whistled with an heroic whistle, till the whole sea was troubled by a storm. Then the two pike he had thrown back into the sea came swimming to the shore. "Why dost thou call us, O Ivan Golik?" said they.

"Why should I not call you? The serpent flew over the sea early yesterday morning and dropped in it his daughter's ring. Search for it everywhere. If you find it, I shall remain alive, but if you find it not, know that the serpent will remove me from the face of the earth!"

Then they swam off and searched, nor was there a single corner of the sea where they searched not. Yet they found nothing. At last they swam off to their mother, and told her what a great woe was about to befall. Their mother said to them, "The ring is with me. I am sorry for him, and still more sorry for you, so you may have it." And with that she drew off the ring, and they swam with it to Ivan Golik, and said, "Now we have requited thy service. We have found it, but 'twas a hard task."

Then Ivan Golik thanked the two pike and went on his way. He found the prince weeping, for the serpent had already sent for him twice, and there was no ring. The moment he saw Ivan Golik he sprang to his feet, and said, "Hast thou the ring?"

"Yes, here it is! But look! the serpent himself is coming!"

"Let him come!"

The serpent was already on the threshold as the prince was going out. They ran against each other with their foreheads, and the serpent was very angry. "Where's the ring?" cried he.

"There it is! But I will not give it to thee, but to her from whom thou didst take it."

The serpent laughed. "Very good!" said he, "but now let us go to dinner, for my guests are many, and we have been waiting for thee this long time."

So they went. The prince arrived at the house, where eleven serpents were sitting down to dinner. He saluted them, and then went on to the daughters, and said, as he drew off the ring, "To which of you does this belong?"

Then the youngest daughter blushed and said, "To me!"

"If it be thine, take it, for I sounded all the depths of the sea in searching for it."

All the others laughed, but the youngest daughter thanked him.

Then they all went to dine. After dinner the serpent said to him, in the presence of all the guests, "Well, prince, now that thou hast dined and rested, to thy tasks again! I have a bow of one hundred poods[30] weight. If thou canst bend this bow in the presence of these my guests, thou shalt have my daughter!"

When dinner was over they all lay down to rest, but the prince hastened off as quickly as he could to Ivan Golik, and said, "Now indeed it is all over with us, for he has given me such and such a task."

"Simpleton!" cried Ivan Golik, "when they bring forth this bow, look at it, and say to the serpent, 'I should be ashamed to bend a bow that the least of my servants can bend!' Then call me, and I'll bend the bow so that none other will be able to bend it again."

With that the prince went straight off to the serpent again, and the serpent commanded and they brought the bow, together with an arrow weighing fifty poods. When the prince saw it, he was like to have died of fright; but they put the bow down in the middle of the courtyard, and all the guests came out to look at it. The prince walked all round the bow and looked at it. "Why," said he, "I would not deign to touch a bow like that. I'll call one of my servants, for any one of them can bend such a bow as that!"

Then the serpent looked at the prince's servants one after the other, and said, "Well, let them try!"

"Come forward thou, Ivan Golik!" cried the prince.

And the prince said to him, "Take me up that bow and bend it!"

Ivan Golik took up the bow, placed the arrow across it, and drew the bow so that the arrow split into twelve pieces and the bow burst. Then the prince said, "Did I not tell you? and was I to put myself to shame by touching a bow that one of my servants can draw?"

After that Ivan Golik returned to his fellow-servants, and put the pieces of the broken bow behind his shin-bone; but the prince returned with the serpents into the guest-chamber, and they all rejoiced because he had done his appointed task. But the serpent whispered something in the ear of his youngest daughter, and she went out, and he after her. They remained outside a long time, and then the serpent came in again, and said to the prince, "There is no time for anything more to-day, but we'll begin again early to-morrow morning. I have a horse behind twelve doors; if thou canst mount it, thou shalt have my daughter."

Then they made merry again till evening and lay down to sleep, but the prince went and told Golik. Golik listened to the prince, and said, "Now thou knowest, I suppose, why I took up those pieces of the broken bow, for I could see what was coming. When they lead forth this horse, look at it and say, 'I will not mount that horse lest I put myself to shame. 'Tis with the horse as with the bow, any one of my servants can mount it!' But that horse is no

IVAN GOLIK DREW THE BOW

horse at all, but the serpent's youngest daughter! Thou must not sit upon her back, but I will trounce her finely."

Early in the morning they all arose, and the prince went to the serpent's house to greet them all, and there he saw twenty of the serpent's daughters, but where was the twenty-first? Then the serpent got up and said, "Well, prince, now let us come down into the courtyard; they'll soon bring out the horse, and we'll see what thou dost make of it."

So they all went out and saw two serpents bringing out the horse, and it was as much as the pair of them could do to hold its head, so fierce and strong it was. They led it out in front of the gallery, and the prince walked round it and looked at it. Then said he, "What! did you not say you would bring out a *horse*? Why, this is no horse, but a mare. I will not sit on this mare, for 'twould be to my shame. I will call one of my servants, and he shall mount her."

"Good!" said the serpent, "let him try!"

The prince called forth Ivan Golik. "Sit on that mare," said he, "and trot her about!"

Ivan mounted the mare, and the two serpents let go. She carried him right up among the clouds, and then down again upon the ground she came, with a ringing of hoofs that made the earth tremble. But Ivan Golik took out a fragment of the broken bow, fifty pounds in weight, and trounced her finely. She reared and bucked and carried him hither and thither, but he flogged her between the ears without ceasing. So when she saw that all her prancing and curveting was in vain, she fell to piteously beseeching him, and cried, "Ivan Golik! Ivan Golik! beat me not, and I'll do all thy behests!"

"I have nothing to do with thee at all," said he, "but when thou dost come up to the prince, fall down before him, and stretch out thy legs toward him!"

At this she bethought her for a long time. "Well," cried she at last, "it must be so, there is no doing anything with thee!" So she carried him all over the courtyard, fell down before the prince, and stretched out her legs toward him.

Then said the prince, "Thou seest what a sorry jade it is! And ye would have had me mount such a mare!"

At this the serpent was full of shame, but there was nothing to be said or done. So they went into the garden and sat them down to dinner. The youngest daughter met them there, and they greeted her. The prince could not refrain from looking at her, so fair was she, and now she seemed fairer than ever. Then they sat down and ate, and when the meal was over the serpent said, "Well, prince, after dinner I'll bring all my daughters into the courtyard, and if you can find out the youngest, you may be happy together."

So after dinner the serpent bade his daughters go and dress themselves, but the prince took counsel of Ivan Golik. Ivan whistled, and immediately the gnat came flying up. He told the gnat all about it, and the gnat said, "Thou didst help me, so now I will help thee. When the serpent brings out his daughters, let the prince keep his eyes open, for I will fly on her head. Let him walk round them once, and I will fly round them too. Let him walk round them a second time, and I will fly round them twice also. Let him walk round them a third time, and then I'll settle on her nose, and she will not be able to endure my bite, but will strike at me with her right hand." And with these words the gnat flew off into the house.

Soon afterward the serpent sent for the prince. He went, and there in the courtyard stood the twenty-one daughters. They were as like as peas, their faces, their hair, and their raiment were exactly the same. He looked and looked, but could not tell one from the other. He walked round them the first time, but there was no sign of the gnat. He walked round them the second time, and the gnat came and lit upon her head. Henceforth he never took his eyes off the gnat, and when he had begun to walk round the twenty-one daughters for the third time, the gnat sat on the nose of the youngest, and began to bite her. She brushed it off with her right hand, whereupon the prince said, "She is mine!" and led her to the serpent.

The serpent was amazed, but said, "Since thou hast found out thy bride, we'll wed thee to-day, and all be merry together."

So they made them merry, and that very evening the young couple got their bridal crowns. And they feasted and fired guns, and what else did they not do? But at night, Ivan Golik took the prince aside, and said to him, "Now, prince, see that we go home to-morrow, for they mean us no good here. And now, listen to me! I beg thee tell not thy wife the truth of the matter for seven years. However caressing she may be, thou shalt not let her ears know the truth, for if thou *dost* tell her the truth, both thou and I shall perish!"

"Good!" said he. "I will not tell my wife the truth."

Next morning the young men arose and went to the serpent, and the prince took leave of his father-in-law, and said he must be going home.

"But why off so soon?" said the serpent.

"Nay, but I must go," said he.

Then the serpent gave the youth a banquet, and they sat down and ate and made merry, and after that he departed to his own tsardom. And the prince thanked Ivan Golik for all that he had done for him, and made him the first of his counsellors. Whatever Ivan Golik said was performed throughout the realm, while the Tsar had only to sit on his throne and do nothing.

So the young prince dwelt with his wife for a year or two, and in the third year a son was added to them, and the heart of the prince was glad. Now one day he took his little son in his arms, and said, "Is there anything in the wide world that I like better than this child?" When the princess saw that the heart of her spouse was tender, she fell a-kissing and caressing him, and began asking him all about the time when they were first married, and how he had been able to do her father's commands. And the prince said to her, "My head would long ago have been mouldering on the posts of thy father's palace had it not been for Ivan Golik. 'Twas he who did it all and not I."

Then she was very wrath. But she never changed countenance, and shortly afterward she went out.

Ivan Golik was sitting in his own house at his ease, when the princess came flying in to him. And immediately she drew out of the ground a handkerchief with gold borders, and no sooner had she waved this serpentine handkerchief, than Ivan fell asunder into two pieces. His legs remained where they were, but his trunk with his head disappeared through the roof, and fell seven miles away from the house. And as he fell he cried, "Oh, accursed one! did I not charge thee not to confess! Did I not implore thee not to tell thy wife the truth for seven years! And now I perish and thou also!"

He raised his head and found himself sitting in a wood, and there he saw an armless man pursuing a hare. He pursued and pursued it, but though he caught it up, he couldn't catch it, for he had no arms. Then Ivan Golik caught it and they fell out about it. The armless one said, "The hare is mine!"--"No," said Ivan Golik, "it is mine!" So they quarrelled over it, but as one had no legs and the other had no arms, they couldn't hurt one another. At last the armless one said, "What is the use of our quarrelling? Let us pull up that oak, and whichever of us pitches it farthest shall have the hare."

"Good!" said Legless.

Then Armless kicked Legless up to the oak, and Legless pulled it up and gave it to Armless. Then Armless lay down on the ground and kicked the oak with his feet three miles off. But Legless threw it seven miles. Then Armless said, "Take the hare and be my elder brother!"

So they became brothers, and made a wagon between them, and fastened ropes to it, and while Armless dragged it along Legless drove it. On they went till they came to a town where a Tsar lived. There they went up to the church, and planted themselves with their wagon in the place of beggars, and waited till the Tsarivna came up. And the Tsarivna said to her court lady, "Take this money, and give it to those poor cripples."

The lady was about to go with it when Legless said, "Nay, but let the Tsarivna give it to us with her own hands."

Then the Tsarivna took the money from her court lady and gave it to Legless. But he said to her, "Be not angry, but tell me, now, wherefore art thou so yellow?"

"God made me so," answered she, and then she sighed.

"No," replied Legless. "I know why thou art so yellow. But I can make thee once more just as God made thee."

Now the Tsar had heard them speaking, and the words of the cripples moved him strangely. So he had the armless man and the legless man in the wagon brought to him, and said to them, "Do as you are able."

But Legless said, "O Tsar! let the Tsarivna speak the truth, and confess openly how she became so yellow!"

Then the father turned to his daughter, and she confessed and said, "The serpent flew to me, and drew my blood out of my breast."

"When did he fly to thee?" they asked.

"Just before dawn, when the guards were sleeping, he came flying down my chimney. In he came flying, and lay down beneath the cushions of my couch."

"Stop!" cried Legless; "we'll hide in the straw in thy room, and when the serpent comes flying in again, thou must cough and wake us."

So they hid them in the straw, and just as the guards had ceased knocking at the doors as they went their rounds, sparks began to flash beneath the straw roof, and the Tsarivna coughed. They rushed up to her, and saw the serpent already nestling beneath the cushions. Then the Tsarivna leaped out of bed; but Armless lay down on the floor and kicked Legless on to the cushions, and Legless took the serpent in his arms and began to throttle it. "Let me go! let me go!" begged the serpent, "and I'll never fly here again, but will renounce my tithes."

But Legless said, "That is but a small thing. Thou must carry us to the place of healing waters, that I may get back my legs and my brother here his arms."

"Catch hold of me," said the serpent, "and I'll take you, only torture me no more."

So Legless clung on to him with his arms and Armless with his feet, and the serpent flew away with them till he came to a spring. "There's your healing water!" cried he.

Armless wanted to plunge in straightway, but Legless shrieked, "Wait, brother! Hold the serpent tight with your legs while I thrust a dry stick into the spring, and then we shall see whether it really is healing water."

So he thrust a stick in, and no sooner had it touched the water than it was consumed as though by fire. Then the pair of them, in their rage, fell upon that false serpent and almost killed him. They beat him and beat him till he cried for mercy. "Beat me no more!" cried he; "the spring of healing water is not very far off!" Then he took them to another spring. Into this they also dipped a dry stick, and immediately it burst into flower. Then Armless leaped into the spring and leaped out again with arms, whereupon he pitched in Legless, who immediately leaped out again with legs of his own. So they let the serpent go, first making him promise never to fly to the Tsarivna again, and then each thanked the other for his friendship, and so they parted.

But Ivan Golik went again to his brother the prince, to see what had become of him. "I wonder what the princess has done to him?" thought he. So he went toward that tsardom, and presently he saw not very far from the roadside, a swineherd tending swine; he was tending swine, but he himself sat upon a tomb. "I'll go and ask that swineherd what he's doing there," thought Ivan Golik.

So he went up to the swineherd, and, looking straight into his eyes, recognized his own brother. And the swineherd looked at him, and recognized Ivan Golik. There they stood for a long time looking into each other's eyes, but neither of them spoke a word. At last Ivan Golik found his voice: "What!" cried he. "Is it thou, O prince, who art feeding swine? Thou art rightly served! Did I not bid thee, 'Tell not thy wife the truth for seven years'?"

At this the prince flung himself down at the other's feet, and cried, "O Ivan Golik! forgive me, and have mercy!"

Then Ivan Golik raised him up by the shoulders and said, "'Tis well for thee that thou art still in God's fair world! Yet wait a little while, and thou shalt be Tsar again!"

The prince thereupon asked Ivan Golik how he had got his legs back again, for the princess had told him how she had cut Ivan Golik in two. Then Ivan Golik confessed to him that he was his younger brother, and told him the whole story of his life. So they embraced and kissed each other, and then the prince said, "'Tis high time I drove these swine home, for the princess doesn't like being kept waiting for her tea."

"Well," said Ivan Golik, "we'll drive them back together."

"The worst of it, brother, is this," said the prince. "Dost thou see that accursed pig that leads the others? Well, he will go only up to the gate of the sty, and there he stands fast as if rooted to the ground, and until I kiss his bristles he will not move from the spot. And all the time the princess and the serpents are sitting in the gallery at tea, and they look on and laugh!"

But Ivan Golik said, "It needs must be so! Kiss it again to-day, and to-morrow thou shalt kiss it no more!"

Then they drove the swine up to the gates, and Ivan Golik looked to see what would happen. He saw the princess sitting in the gallery with six serpents drinking tea, and the accursed pig stuck fast in the gate, and stretched out its legs and wouldn't go in. The princess looked on and said, "Look at my fool driving the swine, and now he is going to kiss the big boar!"

So the poor fellow stooped down and kissed its bristles, and the pig ran grunting into the courtyard. Then the princess said, "Look! he has picked up from somewhere an under-herdsman to help him!"

The prince and Ivan Golik drove the pigs into their sty, and then Ivan Golik said, "Brother, get me twenty poods of hemp and twenty poods of pitch, and bring them to me in the garden." And he did so. Then Ivan Golik made him a huge whip of the twenty poods of hemp and the twenty poods of tar. First he twined tightly a pood of hemp, and tarred it well with a pood of pitch; round this he plaited another pood of hemp, and tarred that also with another pood of pitch, till he had used up the whole forty. By midnight his task was done, and then he laid him down to sleep. But the prince had gone to sleep long before in the pig-sty.

Early in the morning they rose up again, and Ivan Golik said to him, "Up till to-day thou hast been a swineherd, and after to-day thou shalt be a prince again; but first let us drive the swine into the field."

"Nay, but," said the prince, "the princess has not yet come out upon the balcony to drink tea with the serpents, and see me kiss the pig before it goes out, as is her wont." Ivan Golik said to him, "We will drive the swine out this time too, but it will not be thou but I who shall kiss the big boar."

"Good!" said the prince.

And now the time came for the swine to be driven away, and the princess came out on the balcony to drink tea. They took the swine out of the sty, and the pair of them drove the beasts before them. When they reached the gate the leading pig stuck fast in the gateway, and wouldn't budge an inch. The princess and the serpents grinned and looked on, but Ivan Golik flicked his heroic whip, and struck the pig one blow that made it fly to pieces. Then all the serpents wriggled off as fast as they could. But she, the accursed one, was in no way frightened, but caught Ivan by the hair of his head. He, however, caught her also by her long locks, and flicked her with his whip till he had flicked all the serpent-blood out of her, and she walked the earth in human guise. So she cast off her serpent nature, and lived happily with her husband. And that's the end of the *kazka*.

FOOTNOTES

[1] *Div.* This ancient, untranslatable word (comp. Latin *deus*) is probably of Lithuanian origin, and means any malefic power.

[2] A folk-tale; Russ. *skazka*, Ger. *Märchen*.

[3] *Kozak*, a Cossack, being the ideal human hero of the Ruthenians, just as a *bogatyr* is a hero of the demi-god type, as the name implies.

[4] A *grivna* is the tenth part of a rouble, about 2½ d. or 2 shillings and sixpence

[5] Russian *Tsarevna*, *i.e.* a Tsar's daughter.

[6] *Pokute*, the place of honour in a Ruthenian peasant's hut, at the right-hand side of the entrance.

[7] A sourish drink.

[8] A little Tsar.

[9] The two fabulous hounds of Ruthenian legend.

[10] Little Wolf.

[11] Little Bear.

[12] *I.e.* Burning bright.

[13] A pood = 40 lb.

[14] *Shulyak* means both *sparrow-hawk* and *push*.

[15] What a little! What a little!

[16] The hare.

[17] Posad, or posag, a bench covered with white cloth on which the bride and bridegroom sat down together.

[18] Hearkener.

[19] Heavysides.

[20] This is a good instance of the modern intrusions in these ancient *kazki*. An angel and a passport in the same tale!

[21] About twopence-halfpenny.

[22] *Lit.* Big billy-goats, the name given by the clean-shaved Ruthenians to their hairy neighbours the Russians.

[23] The wife of a Tsar.

[24] Hungarian soldier.

[25] *I.e.* a forest where treasure is hidden.

[26] Prayers lasting forty days.

[27] A *karbovanets* is about four shillings.

[28] Wedding-cakes of the shape of pine-cones.

[29] Naked.

[30] A pood = forty pounds.

Abela Publishing

republishing

YESTERDAY'S BOOKS

For

TODAY'S CHARITIES

www.AbelaPublishing.com

R. Nisbet Bain

CPSIA information can be obtained at www.ICGtesting.com
Printed in the USA
LVOW122051090713

342084LV00001B/143/P